Children
of the
Mist

a sequel to Starquest

by

Hywela Lyn

Children of the Mist

Cover Art by *Tamra Westberry*

The Wild Rose Press
PO Box 706
Adams Basin, NY 14410-0706
Visit us at www.thewildrosepress.com

Publishing History
First Faery Rose Edition, 2009
Print ISBN 1-60154-557-6

Published in the United States of America

She kept climbing, losing all track of time.

She stopped to rest. She'd had little sleep and not bothered to eat before she left the camp, and hunger and exhaustion took their toll. All at once she sniffed the air. Clouds of bitter-smelling smoke drifted in a haze above her. She turned her head to one side and concentrated on climbing as swiftly as she could without losing her footing.

It was almost a shock when at last she reached the rim. She eased herself onto the icy ground, and sat for a few moments to catch her breath. Smoke hung in the air and it was obvious there had recently been a fight with power weapons.

Vidarh! Vidarh, are you here?

No answer. Nothing but silence. Abandoning caution, she adjusted her flare to full beam and swung around, stretching her arm and illuminating the ground before her. Suddenly she stood rigid. Over to her right, a large black mound, obviously the Salmaran, or what was left of her, lay inert and lifeless, face downward.

She looked all around, flashing the light on her wrist, straining her eyes for some sign of Vidarh, while calling to him in her mind. She walked away from the Salmaran woman's body, and at last spotted Vidarh lying a considerable distance away.

His arms were flung out away from his sides, his fingers clenched around the butt of his blaster, his garments half covered in snow. She could detect no life-signs.

She ran toward him. Tears spilled down her cheeks and it seemed as if her heart would break.

Reviews for *Starquest*

"...Science fiction novels generally follow one of three themes, and this one is a perfect example of the adventure theme. The heroine is on a quest for her true love, and she travels throughout space in search of him. Along the way, she has many adventures, which teach her things she needs to know about herself and her companions...I quickly became engrossed in Jess's adventures and finished the book in one sitting." ~Fallen Angel Reviews

"...*Starquest* takes the reader onto an awesome galactic journey. The characters are strong and convincing. Jess is a courageous woman who brings so much life to the story. I love her bravery and determination. One will not find a dull moment with this story; it is loaded with action from beginning to end. With secrets, passion and an incredible amount of trust, Jess, Kerry and Dahll learn quickly the true value of where the heart lies. Hywela Lyn weaves a romance that is truly out of this world, as the reader grasps hold and hangs on tightly for the exciting ride of their life." ~Coffee Time Romance

"Adventure, suspense and nail-biting battles so realistic you can smell the blaster fire comprise this sequel to Hywela Lyn's debut novel, *Starquest*. *Children of the Mist* is more than a romance tale. It's a moving story packed with powerful emotions of ruthless vengeance, blood-chilling terror—and personal sacrifice. This unforgettable book is one I recommend as a keeper!"
~Miss Mae, author of *See No Evil, My Pretty Lady* from The Wild Rose Press

Dedication

This book is dedicated to the memory of
John Evans and Grace Davies,
two very special people in my life, who gave me
the encouragement to follow my dreams.
One day we'll meet again, beyond
'the Rainbow Bridge.'

Chapter One

The message from Gladsheim had been clear. Earth Colony Niflheim was in danger.

The rider shivered and drew his long coat more closely around him. His pony lowered its head against the wind, picking its way over the snow-covered plain. Vidarh knew he was not alone on this journey—he sensed the presence of others, all making their way to Gladsheim from various parts of the world.

Without warning, a mind connected with his, as sweet as the tinkle of tiny bells.

Greetings, Vidarh of the House of Ragnak, this is Tamarith of the House of Yarvi. I have been assigned to guide you to our fair city. You have come a long way to be with us, and we, the inhabitants of Gladsheim, thank you.

Relieved, he swiftly telepathed his response. *Greetings Tamarith. I look forward to meeting you and the others soon.*

The rest of your journey is not easy, she replied, *but we will guide you. When you reach the other side of the mountain we will be waiting to take you to Gladsheim.*

As the voice drifted out of his mind, Vidarh found himself looking forward to meeting her. He wondered if she was as pleasant to look at as her voice had sounded in his head. He had indeed come a long way, and not without cause. He allowed himself a wry smile as he thought of his farewell to his family. His father had made it plain he was the best member of the family to go. Not because the old man felt Vidarh had any special qualities, but simply because he was more easily spared than any of his siblings. Vidarh might not be adept at farming, but one day-—one day, he'd find a way of making his father proud of him.

Although concerned about the threat to Niflheim, he'd welcomed the chance to leave the constraints of the farmstead and looked forward to the journey. It would be good to have some time to himself. The only drawback being that at Gladsheim he would have to endure the company of a multitude of people he did not know. However, it would only be for a day or two, and then he could take his time on the return home, enjoying his solitude again.

The ice-cold mist swirled like a living creature, driven by the wind. Vidarh glanced behind him. The distant mountains were almost hidden, their summits mantled in thick cloud. Somewhere an icecat howled, its mournful cry echoing through the mountains and sending ghostly fingers racing up and down his spine. Ahead lay a dense forest, and beyond it, the place he sought.

The trail through the trees led ever upward, and the sure-footed pony snorted and panted with the exertion. The mist blotted out much of the light from Niflheim's two suns. Although a faint eerie glow from the red giant managed to filter through, it did nothing to make the journey easier or the path between the massive trunks clearer. Without guidance from the young woman from Gladsheim, Vidarh might have feared losing the way.

When at last the trees thinned out, he found himself on a high plateau. Before him loomed a towering cliff, studded with the mouths of several caves. He dismounted and stood still, emptying his mind of all thoughts.

If you have reached the caves, you will need to leave your pony and continue on foot.

Guided by Tamarith, Vidarh stopped before the first and largest cave. He would need some form of illumination. From his pack he drew a torch, which he lit and wedged into a crack in the rock.

Unsaddling the pony, he turned it loose. The animal, descended from stock genetically engineered to withstand the harsh conditions, and brought with the first settlers to Niflheim, was fit and hardy. It would have no problem foraging for itself until his return.

With a resolute set to his shoulders, Vidarh retrieved his torch and made his way into the cave. Just inside the mouth, he found a hollow behind a rock in which to hide the saddle and bridle. At least it would be safe and dry there, so long as no hungry rodent decided to nibble at it. He strapped on his pack, containing a change of clothing and a few personal items, and set off along a narrow passageway at the back of the cavern.

Tamarith directed him along the various twists and turns of the labyrinth. At first, the going was easy. The walls of rock gave off a soft, diffuse luminescence, augmenting the light from his torch.

After walking for so long he began to think the tunnel he followed led nowhere, the luminosity grew stronger, and the passage opened out into a large amphitheatre. The light reflected back from the walls revealed seats, formed out of pale green stone, arranged in tiers forming a semi-circle. At one end was a pool, shimmering in the soft light. Multi-colored stalactites glistened like jewelled candelabra from the roof of the cave. At the far end was a high dais flanked on each side by another passage.

Vidarh paused for only a moment to take in the beauty around him. He was familiar with the Conference Chamber of the community of Gladsheim. His mind had been there many times but this was the first time he had physically entered the place.

Instructed to take the left fork, he progressed along the labyrinths, noting the downward slope of the passage. Occasionally, when he came to a branch in the tunnel, he would stop and listen to Tamarith's voice in his mind as it guided him along the right path.

You don't have far to go. I will keep sending you the directions. You should be near the river now.

Yes. I hear it up ahead.

Be careful. We had heavier than usual snowstorms last winter. With the coming of spring, the melting snow and ice has swelled the volume of water.

Vidarh made his way along the tunnel, partly guided by his telepathic link with Tamarith, and partly by his own senses. Eventually it widened out into a large cave, through which the underground river roared as it cut its way through the mountain.

On the shingle of the boulder-strewn shore, several small boats bobbed against their moorings. After ensuring his pack was securely fastened around his waist, he climbed into one, and lashed the torch to the prow. He cast off, and took up the paddle. The river bore the craft along at a tremendous rate and it needed all his skill and attention to save the craft from dashing against the rocks. He'd heard about the fabled river of Mimir, but this was not the tranquil stream of his imagination.

The walls still reflected a phosphorescent glow. Vidarh noticed several gigantic, human-like statues on the banks as he passed, but had no time to contemplate or admire them. Rounding a bend, he came upon a wall of water ahead, cascading from the roof in a fury of white froth. The torrent boiled and raced. He gritted his teeth as he headed into the maelstrom.

There was no way he could control the boat's frantic motions as it heaved and bucked like an unbroken colt. He threw down the paddle, gripped the sides of the vessel, and sent a desperate message through the ether.

Tamarith, I'm in trouble. Please—send me images of your location, quickly. I need to know what it looks like where you are.

The raging current tossed the boat around with relentless fury. All Vidarh's attention focussed on maintaining contact with Tamarith, and even his finely-tuned powers could not prevent the craft from capsizing. Gasping as he hit the icy flood, he struck out with his arms in desperation, and tried to keep the watery demons from pulling him under.

Tamarith!

Into his head came a shimmering picture of mountains and a snowy plain beyond, like the one he had recently crossed. A path before the mouth of a cave wound down the declivity to the plain. He closed his eyes and forced himself to concentrate on the image, while trying to keep his head above the water.

The mountains and the plain solidified in his mind. He saw a group of people gathered at the entrance to the cave, halfway down the craggy slope. Four sturdy ponies stood tethered a short distance away.

Vidarh struck a barrage of water with a force that winded him. Myriad rainbow colours flashed before his eyes. For a nanosecond, he sped through a vortex of black nothingness, sucked through the eye of a raging whirlwind. He hit hard ground and rolled over onto his side. A few moments passed before he could catch his breath and scramble to his feet. He stood in embarrassment, aware of the slightly shocked expressions on the faces of the three people gathered before him.

Welcome, Vidarh. Not quite how we were expecting you to arrive.

The young woman, at whose feet he had fallen, was pleasing to look at, even if her expression was one of bemusement. He'd formed a vague picture in his mind and thought she would be attractive, although he had not expected her to be so stunning. Large, dark eyes framed with feathery lashes lit up her delicate features. Thick black hair in a long braid reached almost to her feet, and the close-fitting riding gear she wore emphasised a petite, shapely figure.

Tamarith smiled, an action that made her seem even lovelier, and extended her fingers in the Nifl custom. *How did you do that?* The question whispered in his mind, and he sensed no one else heard it.

I'll tell you later, he telepathed, also withholding his reply from the others. *I'm not entirely sure myself, I've only managed very short distances previously.* He touched her fingers in return and glanced at a neatly bearded figure and an elderly man standing next to him, who repeated the gesture.

My brother, Gullin. And this is one of our elders, Liftrar, Tamarith informed him as they completed the polite ritual of greeting. *I think we should make for Gladsheim. You must be weary after your journey. Not to mention, wet,* she added with another smile.

Vidarh nodded and she led him over to one of the ponies and held its head while he mounted. With a lithe movement, she stepped into the saddle of her own steed. She waited while the other two climbed aboard theirs, then led the way down the mountainside.

The sure-footed ponies picked their way along the narrow mountain path and Vidarh shivered against the sharp wind, his sodden clothes clinging to him, heavy and uncomfortable, chilling him even further. On reaching the foot of the mountain they urged the ponies into a mile-eating gallop, the exhilarating pace lifting his spirits and making him less aware of his discomfort.

He knew there were questions Tamarith wanted to ask. Every now and then, he caught fragments of her curiosity, and that of the others. However, he merely projected back to her that he would explain once they reached Gladsheim and he'd changed into dry clothes.

At last, Gladsheim came into view. Vidarh drew in his breath. The city was even more beautiful than the stories had led him to believe. The mist, which still swirled over the mountains, had not yet reached the settlement. The setting suns cast a golden glow, suffused with touches of pink and crimson. Elegant houses, ranged around a long, narrow lake beneath snow-capped peaks, stood bathed in the ethereal light. Mosaic paths wound between tinkling fountains, and shrubs and flowers grew in profusion, despite the fine sprinkling of snow on the ground.

Vidarh was still gazing around in awe, when Gullin came to his pony's head and held the bridle for him to dismount.

Come, you must be tired after your journey. You need to change and then we'll eat, and you can meet everyone.

Vidarh was happy to alight from the saddle and hand the reins to a girl, who also held Tamarith's pony. As she and a young man led their mounts away, Vidarh followed Gullin and Tamarith across the delicate bridge, which spanned the lake. Unseen bells tinkled, the sound drifting on the slight wind, and the bridge itself coruscated with all the colours of the spectrum, in the radiance of the two sunsets.

When they reached the far side, Tamarith led him to one of the houses overlooking the lake.

I'll take you to your room. You can bathe before

we have our meal.

****

Refreshed after a long soak in the warm bathing pool, Vidarh donned the clean clothing laid out ready for him. The garments he'd been wearing, and the change of clothing he'd brought, were drying at a safe distance from the cheery fire in the hearth. Everything he had heard about the House of Yarvi's hospitality was well-founded. Gullin and Tamarith could not have made him feel more at home.

Looking around in approval at the spacious room allocated to him, he checked his appearance in the mirror opposite the bed. The hazel eyes that stared back had lost their customary brightness and held the weariness of one who had travelled for many days. Vidarh could do nothing about that but at least he could try to make up for his less-than-dignified arrival by looking as presentable as possible. He ran a comb through his hair in an attempt to tame the unruly curls, which he restrained with a leather band around his head. Tucking the borrowed and slightly too-short breeches into his boots, he tweaked his also-borrowed tunic and forced a smile. He assumed they belonged to one of Tamarith's brothers.

Downstairs, in the vast dining hall, Tamarith smiled and showed him to his seat. While the steaming dishes were brought to the great dining table, she introduced him to the rest of her family. He also met the other guests, as well as Helva and Narvi, the girl and boy who cared for the family's ponies.

When Tamarith sat down beside him, he smiled at her with a feeling akin to relief. Hers was a comparatively familiar face among all the unfamiliar ones. It was also an extremely attractive one.

I've never seen so many people in one place. Sleipnir, where I come from, is a very small community.

There are several hundred people in this hall. They're residing with anyone who is able to find the room to accommodate them, Tamarith replied. *More are expected before tomorrow. Gullin and I have been sending messages for many days. Those who can't be found lodgings in Gladsheim itself will be housed in the outlying hamlets and villages.*

Vidarh nodded and did his best to make polite conversation, although he found it difficult to relax among so many people. Rhenn and Melind, the sixteen-year-old brother and sister of his hosts, were as outgoing and friendly as their older siblings. Melind's smile and ready laughter did much to put him at ease.

A tension lay in the air, however, that even the excellent meal and light-hearted conversation could not dispel. There was a reason for their presence here that went far deeper than the opportunity for a pleasant social gathering.

When they finished eating, Gullin and Tamarith rose and Gullin looked around at the guests assembled at the huge table.

My friends, many of you have travelled far to be here. Thank you for coming. Tomorrow the others should arrive, and then we will combine our minds and try to reach the one person who may be able to help us.

Chapter Two

Vidarh awoke to find the early rays of both suns illuminating his room. A restful night's sleep had dispelled the previous day's weariness and he felt invigorated. He opened the window and breathed in the cool air, fragrant with the smell of conifers, then descended the ornate staircase to the dining hall.

He was not the first to rise. Many had already taken their seats at the table. Gullin was engaged in conversation with a pretty, fair-haired young woman holding a small child in her arms. As Vidarh hesitated by the door, Gullin came across to him.

Good morning, I trust you slept well.

I did, and I thank you and your family for your hospitality.

Gullin waved a hand in a gesture of dismissal. *Not at all. We're only too pleased to have you with us. You haven't met all of my family yet. This is Thamri, my wife, and our daughter, Freya.* Thamri smiled and held out her hand. Vidarh touched fingertips and nodded politely.

First we will eat. Then, when everyone is gathered together, I will explain the situation as I see it, Gullin told him. *You will also meet some of our friends who weren't around when you arrived last night.*

As soon as the meal was finished and the guests left the table, Vidarh spotted Tamarith making her way toward him, with an air of purpose in her stride. This morning she wore a long, elegant crimson gown, a narrow black girdle encircling her tiny waist, with sandals on her feet. Her hair hung loose, rippling around her ankles.

She was unlike any woman he had known—and it wasn't only her beauty that intrigued him. She had a remoteness about her too, despite her pleasant manner, and he had a feeling there was something she was hiding. Something he sensed she felt strongly enough about to deliberately keep shielded, even though it was inherent in their very natures that no telepath on Niflheim would ever pry, unbidden, into the mind of another.

Good morning, Vidarh, it looks as if we're going to have beautiful day.

It certainly does. Given the curious look in her eye, Vidarh was sure Tamarith wanted more from him than small talk.

I would like to talk to you before Gullin calls us all together, if you can spare a few minutes.

Of course, Vidarh agreed as he followed her outside and walked with her along the mosaic path beside the banks of flowers that edged the lake.

****

Tamarith stopped and gazed for a moment across the water. The G-type sun, now fully risen, caused the lake to shimmer like a veil of golden silk, with scarcely a ripple disturbing its calm. The pastel-colored walls of the graceful buildings on the shore reflected the glow of both suns. In the distance, the mountains encircling the settlement reached high into the cerulean sky. The swirling mist that hid their summits was as much a part of Niflheim as the earth upon which she and Vidarh stood.

She sensed his mind discreetly touch hers and realized he was staring at her keenly. She turned back to face him, returning his questioning glance and studying him in turn.

Taller than average, and broad-shouldered, today he wore a sleeveless, belted leather shirt over thick breeches, with long, icecat-wool lined boots. His upper arms were well muscled, his skin tanned as if he were used to working outdoors. His curly, dark auburn hair, kept away from his face with a plain leather band, reached almost to his shoulders. It caught the sun's rays and gleamed like the polished dark red wood of the trees that flanked the feet of the mountains.

She took in his clear, hazel eyes, with their friendly twinkle, the long, straight nose, strong jaw line and smiling mouth. He would have been fighting off the local unattached young women if the situation they found themselves in were not so serious.

Not that she was particularly interested in his looks, or those of any other man, for that matter.

No, something else about Vidarh of Ragnak excited her curiosity.

It's about yesterday...

I thought it might be. Vidarh's lopsided smile looked rather half-hearted. *I realize it was not the most dignified way for a guest to arrive. I rather expected to have to explain it to your brother.*

She allowed her own faint smile. It was just as well she had shielded her thoughts of a moment ago. Vidarh was very perceptive.

Gullin has a great deal on his mind at the moment and is probably more polite than I am. I'm just curious. Forgive me if it sounds like I'm prying. I mean...teleportation? Levitation is one thing, but not many people can actually teleport.

I didn't know I could, myself, until recently. I used to do short 'hops' as a boy and thought it was something everyone did. It was only when I realized the other children of my age didn't teleport that I began to think there was something wrong with me and stopped doing it.

Vidarh paused, looking at her with eyes that did

not lose their sparkle, although a shadow crossed his face.

I'm afraid I'm a disappointment to my father, as it is. I've never been very good around the farm, apart from caring for the ponies, and he believes telepathy for communication, and telekinesis for lifting heavy equipment, are the only mental accomplishments we should concern ourselves with.

After another slight hesitation, he went on, *a little while ago, I was out in the mountains when a storm blew up. I started back down the mountainside, but the blizzard grew more fierce and I knew I wouldn't make it. Although I could have telepathed to my family for help, I didn't want to put them in danger as well. I closed my eyes and visualized my homestead, wishing I could be safely home...and suddenly, there I was. I realized if I could 'see' in my mind, the place where I wanted to go, I could will myself there with the power of my thoughts.*

He glanced at her, with a wry expression in his eyes. *I've been secretly practising over short distances ever since, but yesterday is the furthest I've travelled in this manner. I couldn't have done it if you hadn't sent me the images of where you were, though.*

He smiled again, that crooked smile which was infectious, and she couldn't help returning it.

She allowed her eyes to meet his for a moment, before she quickly lowered them again. *I was caught out on the mountains in a storm myself once, when I was very young. It didn't teach me to teleport though.*

Oh? What happened?

I strayed outside the settlement despite my parents' warnings not to wander too far from home. I was gathering wildflowers when I saw an insect with the most beautifully colored wings I'd ever seen. I followed it, climbing higher and higher up the mountain track. I didn't notice how far below me the settlement was, or how the clouds were building up and the sky darkening. When a sudden blizzard hit, I found an overhanging outcrop of rock with a fissure below, deep enough for me to shelter inside.

Vidarh's expression was sympathetic. *You must have been very frightened. How old were you?*

Only about six or seven, I think. I crouched at the back of the crevice, as the storm increased, while the wind drove the snow past the entrance. When at last it died down, darkness had fallen, and I realized how alone I was. I telepathed for help, and I can still remember my relief when I contacted Gullin and my father and they came to rescue me. At *the time, it was the furthest I'd ever tried to transmit a message. Since then I've always been afraid of being alone in the dark.*

She glanced at him, feeling a little foolish. *I suppose that sounds silly—to be scared of the dark?*

Vidarh gave her a searching look, that momentarily made her feel exposed, as if she'd revealed too much of herself.

Of course not, he reassured her, *not after such an experience. Although I wouldn't have imagined you as someone afraid of anything much. But then most people are frightened of something.*

Does that include you?

He was silent for a moment and she wondered if she had been too inquisitive.

Then Vidarh again gave her a slow smile. There was something very appealing about that slightly crooked smile. Their eyes met and she had a fleeting sense of sadness, or perhaps loneliness, even, as his thoughts touched hers for the briefest of moments. Unaccountably she felt her cheeks begin to flush, but she held his gaze and forced herself to smile back, reassuringly.

I hate crowds, he went on. *I always feel uncomfortable with large groups of people, which is why I'm much more at home in the mountains with only my pony for company.*

And yet you came to Gladsheim, knowing how many people were going to be here?

Vidarh shrugged a reply, obviously reluctant to discuss the matter.

How many other people know? she asked, after a moment. *About you being able to teleport, I mean.*

He shook his head. *You're the first I've told. I haven't even mentioned it to my family.*

Why not? It's not as if it's something to be ashamed of.

Again Vidarh shrugged. I'm not sure. Ours is a small community. I just felt...I don't know, *'different' somehow and I didn't want to be. I knew my father wouldn't approve—*

But that's silly. A gift like that is something to be proud of. In Gladsheim it would be encouraged—nurtured, Tamarith began, but just then, Gullin called them to join the group on the other side of the lake.

****

Along the edge of Lake Forseti, the inhabitants of Niflheim stood several deep. Tamarith knew some had arrived during the night and others had reached Gladsheim early that morning. Many more gathered at the edge of the great snow plain they had ridden over the previous day.

Although normally such a large crowd would have assembled in the great Conference Chamber, even that would not have been big enough to hold all the people who had now congregated in the settlement of Gladsheim. Most of them would have ridden or walked to be here, but she wondered if any of them might have teleported, or was Vidarh the only one?

The subject fascinated her, and she intended to ask him more questions as soon as she could.

She joined Gullin and Liftrar, who stood on the Rainbow Bridge, from which they could be seen by the assembled crowd.

Gullin cast his gaze over the assembled group. *My friends*, he began, *first, we thank you all for coming here, especially those of you who have travelled great distances to be with us. The catastrophe threatening our world is something never before seen on Niflheim. Normally, of course, if we need to discuss matters of importance, we would hold a meeting of minds. However, because the situation is so serious, it was felt necessary for as many of us as are able, to gather in one place.* He paused for a moment. *By combining our physical presence, together with the power of our minds, we need to send a message into space. That is why we in Gladsheim—fortunately one of the areas that seems to have escaped the threat—have asked you to come here and join with us. There is only one planet we know of that would have the technology to help us in this emergency, and one person who would have the means to reach them. Together with everyone on Niflheim who is unaffected, we must unite and transmit a message.*

At a signal from Gullin, a number of people moved to join him on the bridge. Everyone joined hands with the person next to them, and closed their eyes in contemplation.

After allowing several moments to elapse, he went on: *There is no guarantee we will reach her, but we must try. We helped her once—perhaps she would be willing to help us in return. We must hope we can reach her, wherever she may be now. Many of you may remember her from when she last visited this planet. Her name is Jestine Darnell.*

Chapter Three

Once again the voices crept into her dreams, and Jess woke in confusion.

The dreams brought with them memories of the time she had visited the planet Niflheim. Memories of how its telepathic inhabitants had helped her to reach out into space, to set out on a course that would lead to adventures she had never imagined, and to love, in the last place she expected to find it.

She remembered 'journeying' in her mind with Gullin, high above the jagged mountains. She recalled hearing 'voices' which were not voices, 'words' which were not words but which she understood, as the Nifls communicated with each other across the void.

Then, it had been different. Hers had been a simple request for information, a plea to help her find the starship, *Destiny*.

Now, there was a sense of urgency in the thoughts that drifted into her mind, something akin to fear. She was sure her friends were in trouble and were asking for her help.

She sat up and shook back the hair that had fallen across her eyes, obscuring her vision like a red mist, and tried to clear her mind.

"Jess, what's wrong?" Dahll Tarron touched the bulkhead and a reassuring light filled the cabin of the *Quest*. Turning, he wrapped his arms around her and kissed the top of her head, then looked into her eyes.

"I'm not sure. It was almost like someone calling to me, in fact there were many voices."

"You were dreaming, sweetheart."

"Perhaps you're right," she murmured, reassured as she always was by her husband's calmness and practicality.

He smiled and kissed her again, holding her close, and she pressed her body against his, inhaling the delicious male scent of him. She smiled back and caressed his face, then wove her fingers through his blond, wavy hair. As he met her gaze, she trembled with a need fuelled by the love that had not diminished in the three years since she had become his Lady.

His own smile turned playfully hopeful, and as his lips trailed from her face, down her neck and shoulder to the curve of her breasts, what had had started as a comforting gesture of affection had become something else entirely. She responded fervently, emptying her mind of everything except the ecstasy of making love with this man with whom she had chosen to spend her life.

Some time later, she lay cradled in his arms, soothed by his steady breathing. She should be sleeping by now. Dahll was both a thorough and considerate lover and there should be no reason for her wakefulness. She was usually deliriously drowsy after their lovemaking, but this time sleep refused to come.

The memories of the voices in her mind returned to haunt her and she knew they had been more than just a dream.

****

Over the next three days the 'voices' increased in strength and clarity. Jess heard them not only when she was in that ethereal state between waking and sleeping, not sure where reality ended and dreams began, but they also whispered to her when she was fully alert, going about her normal routine on board the *Quest*.

She walked across the control deck, and, standing behind Dahll, put a gentle hand on his arm. "Can we talk for a moment?"

Dahll turned from his favourite game of skill with the computer, then froze the programme, and looked at her with an expression of curiosity in his grey, gold-flecked eyes.

"You make it sound serious."

"How do you feel about going back to Niflheim?"

"Niflheim?" I know we always said we'd go back, and I hadn't forgotten...but why now?"

"Why not?"

"Come on," he said, taking both her hands in his. "Out with it. This is because of the 'dreams' you've been having, isn't it?"

"I don't think they're dreams."

"What, then?"

"I think the Nifls are in trouble. I...I sort of sense Tamarith and her people are asking us for help. You remember when Tamarith 'spoke' to you telepathically when we first landed on Niflheim, when we were separated from each other in the caves beyond Gladsheim? She telepathed to tell you I was safe, and guided you to where I was?"

Dahll nodded, still holding her hands.

"Well that's how I hear the 'voices' in my mind. At first they were too faint for me to realize what they were, until the other night, when you thought I was dreaming. They became much clearer then. Now I hear them whenever I close my eyes for a moment, or am not thinking of anything in particular."

Dahll's face wore an expression of concern. "In this sector of space we're about three light years away from Niflheim. That's a fair distance for a telepathic message to reach across."

"But by working together they projected messages across the whole planet and into space and contacted telepaths on the planet Antargonn, when I

19

was searching for the *Destiny*. Couldn't they have done the same again, trying to contact us? We're not much further away from Niflheim now, than Antargonn is to Niflheim."

"There were many telepaths on Antargonn, though." He gave her hands an understanding squeeze. "And we're not telepathic." Jess shook her head. "I know, but Tamarith was able to reach you, and I was always able to receive messages from her very easily. She seemed to have a special gift, to be able to reach out further than anyone else. She taught me a lot about the power of the mind while we were there. I'm sure hers is one of the voices I've been hearing."

She stepped even closer and looked up at him. "If I'm mistaken about the Nifls being in trouble—well, we did say we'd go back to Niflheim one day, so we'll have kept our promise. But supposing I'm right?"

Dahll folded his arms around her and looked deep into her eyes. "Jess, if you really feel the Nifls need our help, then we'd best get there as quickly as we can."

She flashed him a grateful smile. "I knew you'd understand. I've already worked out the co-ordinates. It's just a matter of feeding them into the navigation computer."

Dahll chuckled softly, and Jess gave him an answering grin. It felt presumptuous to have taken his agreement for granted, but she also knew there was very little he could deny her.

****

Jess looked up as Dahll walked on to the Flight Deck. She rose from her customary seat by the scanner screen, her gaze straying back to the brilliant vista of stars it displayed. The nature of hyperspace and the *Quest's* Faster-Than-Light speed made it impossible to observe them in real time in the void of space, and what she saw was a computerised extrapolation. However, this did nothing to detract from their beauty and the fascination they held for her—although just then something else occupied her mind.

"You've had another message?"

"Yes. A few minutes ago. It's always the same thing—they need help." She sighed. "I wish I knew what was going on."

Dahll sat on the low padded seat, and pulled her gently toward him.

Placing his arm around her, he stroked her hair, holding her close. "Well, whatever it is, I reckon they must believe you can help them. According to the computer, we'll be there in another ten hours. There's nothing we can do until then."

"You know what else I'm worried about?"

His expression told her he did. "I can guess. You're worried about what Tamarith's reaction will be when she sees us...together."

"I just wonder how much she knows. They've obviously been concentrating their thoughts on contacting me. I wouldn't think they'd expect to find me on the *Quest*, they'd anticipate I'd have found the *Destiny* by now, and assume you'd returned to Anraat."

"You don't think they'll have picked up something from your thoughts?"

She shook her head. "You know they never try to probe the thoughts of non-telepaths, although," she added with a half smile, "Tamarith seemed to 'sense' quite a lot from us both when we were on Niflheim."

They had decelerated to just under light speed, and were close enough to Niflheim for the planet to show up on their scanners, when the voices abruptly ceased.

"They know we're coming now," Jess told Dahll as they stood together on the Flight Deck. "Or at least," she qualified with a wry smile, "they know *I'm* coming."

"Shall we land the *Quest* on the Plain of Drasil, on the other side of the mountains this time? I don't fancy trekking through the underground caverns again—and we need to save as much time as we can."

"There's no reason why we shouldn't land close to Gladsheim. At least this time we have the advantage of knowing a lot more about the terrain."

"They still haven't told you why they've asked you to come?"

Jess shook her head. "No. All I could get from Tamarith was they're in trouble and need my help."

****

The *Quest* touched down on the vast, snowy expanse of the Drasil Plain, about half a kilometre away from the settlement of Gladsheim. Dahll made haste to set up the elaborate anti-intrusion device, which he had perfected from the rather crude method he had devised several years before. Not that they expected any of the inhabitants of Niflheim to try to steal the ship. The Nifls were a peace-loving and honourable people. Although the *Quest's* sensors had not indicated any other ships in either stationary or synchronous orbit around the planet, in view of the nature of the messages Jess had been receiving it seemed prudent to ensure the ship's safety.

They walked the short distance to the 'City', as the inhabitants of Gladsheim liked to call their settlement. A large crowd waited to greet them. All at once, a young woman detached herself from the group and ran forward. She stopped short a little way off and stood, as if uncertain whether to carry on or remain where she was.

Jess crossed the short distance between them and threw her arms around the girl. "Tamarith, I'm so pleased to see you again!"

Tamarith returned her embrace, then stood back a little. "I was sure you'd come. I knew if we tried hard enough and were able to reach you, you would not let us down." As Dahll reached them in a few, short strides, a faint flush tinged her cheeks. "Dahll—thank you too, for coming."

He stepped forward, and taking her hand, kissed it in the Anraatian manner, which had so captivated Jess when she'd first met him. Jess felt a surge of pride and admiration well up inside her, for the tall, good-looking young man who had stolen her heart and pledged his love to her for all time. She studied Tamarith astutely, wondering how much of her feelings Tamarith was hiding. Then the young woman smiled, and, linking her arm through both Dahll's and Jess's, walked to where the others waited.

A familiar figure stepped across and held out his hand. Jess and Dahll both touched his fingers with theirs, in accordance with the Nifl custom, before Jess embraced him briefly.

"Gullin, it's good to see you again." She glanced at the attractive woman standing by his side and holding a small child.

"Jess, Dahll, this is my wife, Thamri—and Freya, our daughter."

Thamri stepped forward shyly and, still holding the baby with one arm, held out the other to exchange greetings with Dahll and Jess. "Welcome, and thank you for coming. Gullin and Tamarith have both told me a lot about you."

"We're so happy to meet you," Jess said, gazing at the sleeping child in Thamri's arms. "Freya, what a lovely name."

"Named after the Norse goddess of beauty, of ancient Earth legend." Gullin smiled proudly. "For is she not beautiful, like her mother?"

"She certainly is," Jess agreed, stifling the urge to ask if she could hold the baby. Time enough for that, later. She was sure the Nifls had summoned her to Niflheim for reasons other than to meet Gullin's new family.

"Looks like we've all got some catching up to do." She said, looking at Dahll. Gullin turned to allow Rhenn and Melind to greet them, followed by the grey-haired elder, Liftrar. Jess was pleased to note the patriarch looked hardly any older than when she had last seen him. Gullin introduced some of the others, including the young man, Vidarh, from the isolated settlement of Sleipnir. He led the small party to the Rainbow Bridge, and stood with Dahll and Jess on one side of him, Tamarith and Thamri, Rhenn and Melind, on the other.

Gullin held up his hands for attention, and everyone looked at him expectantly. "My friends," he said, "Our request has been answered."

Jess realized he was using speech, rather than telepathy, for the benefit of herself and Dahll. Although the Nifls were capable of projecting their thoughts to anyone, telepath or not, the non-telepath would, of course, be incapable of responding telepathically, so using speech was a simple courtesy.

"Jess and Dahll have come to help us. Go now and rest yourselves. We will explain the situation to our two good friends and tomorrow we will all meet here and discuss what is to be done."

The crowd dispersed. Gullin and Thamri escorted Jess and Dahll to Gullin's home. As they walked, Jess tried to strike up a conversation with Tamarith, who seemed unusually quiet. Jess noted the other woman's glance frequently strayed to Dahll, although she immediately averted her eyes if she saw Jess looking at her. It must have come as a considerable shock to see him again, and to realize he and Jess were pair-bonded. She tried to find a safe topic of conversation.

"How's Dancer? Do you still have him?" She'd grown very fond of the pony she'd ridden on her previous visit to Niflheim.

Tamarith smiled, the sadness leaving her eyes for a moment. "Oh, he's fine, older of course but still very fit and lively. You'll be able to see him tomorrow if you like."

"I'd love to. I know you haven't called us here for a social visit, and I'm sure you'll let us know what it's all about in due course. But I think you and I need to talk as well."

Tamarith nodded and they walked on in silence.

****

The meal was excellent, although not quite as formal as the ones Jess remembered from her previous visit. Afterward they sat in front of a blazing log fire and Jess was delighted when Thamri asked if she would like to hold Freya. As Jess held out her arms, Freya chuckled and waved her little hands in the air, stretching them out toward her. Gently Jess took the chubby baby, rearranging the infant's shawl, and gazed down at her with something approaching awe. An only child herself, she had not had much contact with small children, apart from a year when she had worked at the main medical centre on Phidia.

In the three years since she and Dahll had made their vows to each other, and registered their commitment on Dahll's home planet Anraat, they had spent most of their time in space, on board the *Quest*. There had been little opportunity for thoughts of family or domesticity. She glanced at Dahll and smiled, a soft, almost wistful smile, then caught Thamri's glance and flushed slightly, looking back down at the baby.

Freya giggled and gurgled as Jess rocked her

gently, before falling asleep with a look of peace and contentment on her small face. With some reluctance, Jess handed the child back to Thamri, who placed her once more in her cradle and offered a nod of approval.

"You obviously have the right touch. It's not often she goes to sleep as quickly as that. You'd make a good mother."

"She's a good baby," Jess said, to hide her embarrassment.

"She certainly is." Gullin placed a hand on his wife's shoulder as he looked down at their sleeping daughter. "She sleeps all night and wakes up laughing."

"Yes, and like her father, she is always hungry." Thamri smiled. Jess laughed softly with the others, glad for a lightening of the tension she sensed, coming not from Gullin or his wife, but from Tamarith.

Now that the baby had settled, and Thamri was able to relax for a while, Tamarith and Gullin exchanged glances.

"I think it's time to get down to business." Gullin said. "We've asked you to come here for a reason." His words hung, suspended in the air for a moment, before he went on, "I know this must sound dramatic, but...our people are dying. In a matter of months, most of the population of Niflheim could be wiped out."

Chapter Four

As Gullin paused, Tamarith glanced around the room, and noticed Vidarh standing at the back, away from the others. It almost seemed as if he were distancing himself from them. She bit her bottom lip as she studied him, trying to remain unobtrusive. There was something about him...something that bothered her, which she couldn't quite define. He had a way of looking at her that made her uncomfortable although he was never anything but pleasant. In fact, she had to acknowledge that she rather enjoyed his company.

Her gaze went involuntarily to Dahll. Even taller than Vidarh, his lithe form was lean, and not as muscular. He was strikingly handsome, in a way that was a contrast to Vidarh's dark and rugged good looks. His blond hair had the same tint of gold she remembered, his amazing pale eyes, now filled with concern, were still as capable of making her heart lurch to her stomach. With a sigh, she turned her attention back to Gullin.

"There is a strange malady which afflicts our planet. It is spreading, and all the indications are that it will eventually become a pandemic."

Jess's voice had an edge of shocked amazement. "I thought there weren't any diseases as such on Niflheim, because the climate is too cold for the organisms which cause them to multiply."

"That is true, normally," Gullin agreed. "But we believe this is a particularly virulent virus, which is impervious to the conditions on Niflheim. We have no idea how to deal with it."

"Do you know how or where it started?" Dahll asked.

"It seems to have begun in the region known as Nastrond. It's not a very habitable area. It's on the shores of a vast saltwater lake. Only a few isolated homesteaders manage to eke out a living there." Gullin looked at his sister.

"We first had reports that people were falling ill several weeks ago," Tamarith said, taking up the narrative. "We thought it was an isolated incident. Then the virus began to spread and it became evident people were not just ill, they were dying. She kept her eyes fixed on Jess. "To make it even worse, one of the first symptoms of the disease is that the victims lose their telepathic powers, so it was a while before we realized the scale of the outbreak. Many of our people are traders. We think that may be how it spread, as they travelled across the Burian Sea and moved from settlement to settlement."

Dahll looked surprised. "Then your doctors have not been able to find a cure? I know your medics are very skilled with herbal and natural medicines."

Tamarith shook her head and glanced quickly away. "Our healers have no experience of such an illness. They can treat broken bones and other injuries, and the usual minor ailments that even we succumb to sometimes, but we have never needed to deal with anything like this." Her gaze rested on Jess once more. "Our people have no resistance to it. There's never been even a localised epidemic before, let alone a threatened pandemic. Whatever is causing this must be a mutation that's able to survive the extreme cold and reproduce itself."

"And how can we help?" Jess asked.

"We were wondering—" Tamarith hesitated, still avoiding Dahll's eyes, "we were wondering if...if you could ask the Phidians if it's possible for them to manufacture some sort of vaccine to help us fight this."

"We would not ordinarily ask," Gullin put in. "We realize it's expecting a lot of you, and the Phidians may not want to help. However, we have discussed it with everyone on Niflheim who was still able to contact us. It was felt this was the only option open to us. Without advanced medical help the disease will decimate our people. You may not be able to help us. We will, of course, understand if that is the case."

Jess stood and laid a hand on his arm. "Why would we not wish to help?" she said, her voice husky. "You're our friends—you helped me when I was trying to find the *Destiny*. I'll never forget your kindness then, and I'm sure the Phidians will be willing to help. I don't think finding a cure for whatever is ailing your people will be too difficult for them."

"Thank you. I knew in my heart you would not refuse us." Tamarith swallowed and forced herself to look at Dahll. "What about you Dahll? It's your decision, as well."

"You shouldn't even have to ask," Dahll replied, "I feel the same way Jess does, and I remember your hospitality and help last time we were here, too."

Tamarith smiled her thanks, wishing Dahll's direct gaze did not have such an effect on her. She was sure everyone in the room could hear the thudding of her heart.

"Is there anything else you can tell us about this disease?" The question came from Jess. "Do you know how it originated?"

"We suspect that it is a mutation and was contracted first from the goats kept for milk," Gullin said. As soon as we became aware of what was happening, we decided to ask as many people as possible from the unaffected areas to congregate here, so we could try to contact you."

29

"Have you any idea how the goats became infected in the first place?" Dahll asked.

"None at all. It is a complete mystery. Our animals were all genetically engineered to cope with the conditions here, and brought in cryogenic suspension with the first settlers. There is no likelihood of any inherited diseases having suddenly developed in their descendents."

"The problem is," Tamarith went on, "we don't know how virulent the disease has become. It seems to have developed from nowhere, and mutated, so there is a danger it could spread over the whole planet. According to our physicians, it appears capable of spreading in ways not normally possible in a virus. It also seems to cross species, so even quarantining whole areas of Niflheim won't stop it spreading. The virus could still be dispersed by the wildlife."

"How are we going to demonstrate to the Phidians the type of virus they need to deal with?"

"That's the difficult part, Jess," Gullin stated. "We obviously would not want to put you and Dahll in any danger by asking you to take an infected person on board your ship. Not everyone is susceptible to the illness, though." He paused for a moment. "Those who are infected usually die quickly once the disease takes hold. The few who recover, however, develop a resistance to further infection—and some individuals seem to be immune anyway. One of our physicians, who has that immunity, left for Thorren this morning to bring back samples of living cells from victims of the disease, in sealed containers. We hope the Phidians will be able to identify the virus and perfect an antidote for us."

"I'm sure they will," Jess said, and Tamarith wondered if she were as confident as she sounded. "We'll leave as soon as we can—"

Gullin laid a hand lightly on Jess's shoulder.

"We must wait for the physician to return from Thorren, and it is a three day ride there and back. You might as well rest a little before your journey. We will enjoy having your company for a while longer."

"In that case, we'd be happy to stay for a spell, wouldn't we, Dahll?"

Dahll nodded. "I reckon so; your hospitality is very difficult to refuse."

"Tomorrow we will meet with the others and tell them you've agreed to help us." Tamarith tried to sound casual. "There is one other thing I think you ought to know. It is something that seems to be unconnected with the illness afflicting our people— but in the areas where the sickness has struck, several people have disappeared. And we've been unable to reach them with our telepathy."

****

The two suns had only just risen when Jess awoke. Dahll still slept. After talking with Gullin and his family until late into the night, there had been something she wanted to discuss with Dahll when they finally retired to bed; something she needed to ask him, which was too important to keep until later. Even though this meant they had slept for only a few hours she was now fully alert, diverse thoughts whirling around in her mind.

Very carefully, so as not to wake him, she disentangled herself from his arms, and planted a soft kiss on his lips before dressing. She tiptoed down the stairs leading to the long hallway, and lifted the heavy catch on the wooden door, taking care not to make a noise and disturb the other residents in the house. They were staying with Gullin and Thamri and Jess wondered if the couple had deliberately avoided putting them up in Tamarith's home to avoid any awkwardness.

A thin covering of snow crunched beneath her

31

feet. The breeze sweeping down from the mountains was cold and invigorating. It brought with it the scent of evergreen forests, mingled with that of the hardy blossoms which managed to push up out of the cold earth and reach toward the sunshine.

She stopped for a moment to gaze at the mountains behind her. There was so much of Niflheim she remembered with affection; so much she knew nothing of. She would have loved the opportunity to explore. With a little sigh, she turned and walked over to the barn. Difficult though it might be, she needed to talk with Tamarith.

****

Tamarith swung around as the door opened. She stopped brushing her pony as Jess approached, forcing her mind back to the present. For once, her thoughts had been on someone other than Dahll. She was thinking about Vidarh, or, more accurately, her recent conversation with him. She had often wondered what it would be like to be able to transport oneself from one place to another—instantly.

"'Morning, Tamarith. Isn't it a lovely day?"

"Oh, Jess. Good morning. You've come to see Dancer?"

"I didn't know anyone was here. I just wanted to see him again. I hope it's all right." She rummaged in her pocket and produced the tidbit she'd brought for the pony.

Tamarith hesitated a moment before answering. She felt a little uncomfortable. There was still tension between them—a feeling of unease that had never been there before, and Tamarith knew it was her fault. She watched Jess scratch the pony affectionately behind the ears, as he took the treat from her hand.

"Of course it's all right. I know you grew fond of him when you were here. I'm sure he's pleased to see you again, too. It's been so long. What do you think of Gullin's wife...and the baby?" She knew she was babbling as she tried to break through the awkwardness that had replaced their former ease with each other. "Isn't she the sweetest little thing you've ever seen?"

"She certainly is, and Thamri seems a lovely person," Jess agreed, before giving Dancer a final pat and walking around to the stall where Tamarith stood.

Tamarith ceased the steady brushing of the pony's mane and looked up, not quite able to meet Jess's eyes.

"I hope you don't mind me asking, but...is it very difficult for you, my being here with Dahll?"

Tamarith drew a deep breath and paused before answering. "Have I really been that obvious?"

"You never made any secret of the fact you found him attractive," Jess said gently. "It must have been quite a shock when we turned up together."

"Not a shock, exactly. I sensed his presence when we were trying to reach you. I knew Dahll loved you as soon as I saw the way he looked at you when you first arrived on Niflhcim, together, searching for the *Destiny*. I didn't need to be telepathic to realize that. It didn't stop me hoping, though. Foolish of me, I know."

She turned away briefly before looking back at Jess. "But you told me, that first night, you weren't interested in him. You were searching for Kerry, the man you said you loved. I thought then, when he realized you and he could never be together, Dahll might come to understand how I felt about him and learn to feel the same." She shrugged, and tried to smile, although she knew the result was a little half-hearted. "I should have known he would stay constant in his love for you, even if it had never been

---

returned."

Jess took a step closer to her, and, placing one hand on the pony's flank, put her other on Tamarith's arm.

"I suppose you think I'm very contrary. I was so obsessed with finding the *Destiny* and Kerry, yet here I am, Dahll's *Lady*."

Tamarith allowed herself a slow smile. "I know you're not, Jess. Remember we have linked minds. I've seen your thoughts. But I said you and Dahll would come to be...close, did I not?"

"You did," Jess recalled. "And I thought you meant we would come to be good friends. Which we did...we are. But we went through so much together. We faced terrible danger and so much happened to draw us close. I suppose it was inevitable I should fall in love with him, although it took me a long time to realize it."

"I'm glad." Although it hurt Tamarith to admit it, it was true.

Jess looked at her, an expression of surprise on her face. "Glad?"

Tamarith smiled, although she was aware it did not conceal the pain she felt. "If you'd left him, Dahll would never have loved anyone else. I was only fooling myself to believe he ever would. I know that now."

Wordlessly Jess hugged her, then stood back. "There's someone out there for you too, Tamarith. I'm sure there is."

Tamarith shook her head. "Perhaps. I don't know. I'm not looking." She lowered her head for a moment. "Maybe I'm not meant to find anyone else, and it's up to Gullin to continue our line. And of course, there's still Rhenn and Melind. Perhaps I'm meant to be an old maid aunt, doting on my nephews and nieces."

"I'm sure that's not true," Jess said, taking her

arm. "I can't imagine you never marrying and having a family of your own."

Tamarith wished she could believe her. She did not relish the thought of living her life alone, but she could not imagine meeting anyone who could come anywhere near Dahll in her estimation. The young men of Gladsheim who had so far shown any interest in her made no impression, and she'd learned to keep them at a distance.

They turned to leave the barn, after giving the ponies a final pat. "I'm glad we've had this talk and can still be friends," Jess said, giving Tamarith a brief hug. "I would be sad if I lost your friendship." The warmth of her smile lifted Tamarith's spirits, compelling her to smile back.

"As for not finding anyone else," Jess murmured, "don't give up. I sometimes have premonitions myself, you know."

Tamarith nodded, without conviction. Their talk had lightened the atmosphere between them but seeing Jess and Dahll together and so obviously absorbed in each other, was almost more than she could bear.

****

There was much to do. The many inhabitants of Niflheim who had journeyed to Gladsheim to unite their minds in calling to Jess held frequent gatherings to discuss the progress of the strange affliction that threatened their very existence. They were aware Jess and Dahll had agreed to travel to the planet Phidia, renowned for its great advances in medicine, to enlist the Phidians' help in finding a remedy.

The pair met many of the visitors to Gladsheim with whom they had not previously spoken, and spent time with Vidarh. He kept them enthralled with interesting tales of his distant homeland and Jess decided she liked him. She sensed he was, in some way she could not quite define, different.

On her frequent visits to the stables, Jess struck up an acquaintance with the two youngsters, Helva and Narvi, who cared for most of the settlement ponies. To her delight, she was even able to take a long ride on Dancer, with Dahll and Tamarith.

The physician Gullin had spoken of, Hermot, arrived back at Gladsheim as expected, three days after their arrival. He had brought several tissue samples in case any deteriorated on the journey. After a brief discussion with him, Jess and Dahll transferred the containers to the *Quest's* small medical laboratory, where they would remain in stasis for the journey to Phidia.

Tamarith, together with Gullin and his family, Vidarh and several others, gathered to say farewell and wish them luck on their journey.

"We'll be as swift as we can," Jess assured them. "The *Quest* is fast, and if anyone can find a cure, I'm sure the Phidians will be able to."

As she and Dahll prepared to board the ship, Jess could only hope the Phidians would indeed be able to help her friends, and that her words were not just empty assurances.

****

Niflheim dwindled on the scanner to a small speck, in the vast blackness of space. Dahll placed a hand on Jess's shoulder.

"We'd better prepare for hyper-acceleration."

Jess rose to her feet. "You're right." Preparation for hyper-acceleration entailed administering themselves with an injection of the serum, which Dahll's father had invented to protect the user from the effects of acceleration to Faster-Than-Light speed. Dahll had tested and perfected it during their search for the *Destiny* and the sale of the formula had ensured their wealth and security for the foreseeable future.

As they reached the ship's small Sick Bay the Red Alert rang out, startling them both and sending them racing back to the Flight Deck.

Emergency! On the screen set into the bulkhead, the computer-generated image of an elderly man projected an expression of concern. *Forcefield ahead. Auto-control systems will instigate shutdown of all drives in two minutes and twenty seconds.*

Chapter Five

Vidarh watched the already darkening sky streaked with fingers of flame from the setting suns, until the *Quest* was a faint glimmer of light, scarcely distinguishable from the early evening stars. The echo of the powerful thrusters, as the ship launched itself from the surface of the planet, reverberated in his ears even now. The ground still vibrated beneath his feet, although they stood at a safe distance from the take-off area.

He turned back to Gullin and Liftrar. He noticed Tamarith looked strained, still staring up at the sky, her hands clenched in front of her.

I'm sure Jess and Dahll will be able to get us the help we need. Let's go back to the others, Liftrar telepathed, obviously concerned by Tamarith's expression of anxiety. Vidarh briefly laid what he hoped was a reassuring hand on Tamarith's shoulder. It had not escaped his notice how nervous she acted around Dahll, despite her obvious friendship with Jess. It seemed to him she was thinking about more than the present medical emergency.

They made their way back to the Rainbow Bridge where the crowd waited for them, having watched the departure of the *Quest* from vantage points nearby. Slowly the throng pulled away to allow the elders, and Tamarith and Gullin, to step up onto the bridge. As the rays of the setting suns reflected across the lake, the bridge again lived up to its name. It shimmered in myriad colours, which glowed and sparkled in flashes of light along its whole length, casting fiery reflections upon the water.

Gullin, as usual, took up the position of spokesperson.

Our friends are on their way to the planet we hope has the resources to help us, he began as the murmur of telepathic voices died down. *Thank you all for your assistance in contacting them. There is nothing further we can do now, except wait. Those of you who wish to stay on in Gladsheim are naturally welcome, but if any of you want to return to your homes, then by all means, please do so. We will contact you as soon as we have any news.*

There will, of course, still be limitations on movement from infected areas, but if Jess and Dahll can bring us back a cure, we can then lift all such restrictions. Meanwhile, I am sure you will accept that this is the best way of ensuring the survival of as many of our people as possible.

Gradually the crowd dispersed and Gullin led those who were staying with him, as well as those lodging with Tamarith and her siblings, to his house at the edge of the lake.

Vidarh tagged behind a little, deep in thought. He had come a long way to link his mind with his fellow Nifls in the settlement that was the home of some of the most gifted telepaths on Niflheim. The time-honoured method of communicating over vast distances by uniting minds, enhanced by physical contact, had been the reason for his journey. It was both an enlightening and an exhilarating experience.

He had participated in group-transmissions before, many times, despite his aversion to crowds, but never on such a large scale, or into the vast regions of space. He was as relieved and excited as everyone else when they sensed their messages had been received. However, he'd been reluctant to believe they'd accomplished their objective until the

Quest actually landed and Dahll and Jess stepped out on the Drasil Plain. It pleased him to know he had contributed to their successful contact.

Perhaps this would prove to his father that his second-eldest son wasn't the failure his family seemed to believe he was.

Well he'd done his part, and he would soon have to leave Gladsheim. As he had often been reminded, he had a duty to help his parents run the farmstead even if his heart wasn't in it.

He would miss Tamarith more than he cared to admit. He'd enjoyed the short time they'd spent together, and would have liked the opportunity to get to know her better. She stirred feelings in him that had previously lain dormant, and that in itself was worth exploring.

****

Later, as everyone was leaving the great hall after the evening meal, Gullin turned to Vidarh. *Are you departing tomorrow, or will you be staying on with us for a while?*

I ought to be getting back to Sleipnir. There's always work to do at home, and I have no real excuse for staying here now.

Sleipnir is up in the Northern ridges, isn't it?

That's right. It's a tiny hamlet, only a dozen or so homes. My parents have a farmstead a few miles from Sleipnir itself. The land's fertile enough though and we make a fair living.

I expect your family will be missing you.

Vidarh shrugged. *Perhaps, but I'm no great shakes as a farmer. That's why I volunteered to come. We felt at least one of us should come to give a physical presence and I was more easily spared than any of my brothers.* He smiled ruefully. *I'm afraid my family feels I tend to waste too much time in the woods, 'thinking' and 'experimenting' with my mind, and not enough on practical things.*

It might not be prudent to reveal he believed he was an embarrassment to his family, and always practiced in the solitude of the mountains. He'd decided long ago to develop and refine his particular abilities away from curious eyes. Somehow he had never felt that he really 'belonged' in the environment in which he had been raised. There was something missing from his life, which he knew he would never find in the little settlement of Sleipnir with its outmoded and unprogressive ideas.

Gullin smiled, his thoughts bringing Vidarh back from his reverie. *Things are obviously different in your community. Here your talents would be admired and encouraged. Will you be travelling back with the rest of the villagers?*

Another thing it would probably be tactful not to mention...that he would prefer to return as he had come, alone. *No, I'll travel faster by myself. I was late leaving, and didn't come with the party from Sleipnir, so I might as well make the journey back—*

He stopped abruptly. While they conversed, he had sensed, as if from a vast distance away, a presence, gigantic and powerful, which he had tried to dismiss as merely his imagination. Not for the first time, either. He'd been vaguely aware of something huge, although oddly benign, but beyond his comprehension, just after the *Quest* had landed. He'd pushed it to the back of his mind, assuming he was imagining things.

No doubt it was a combination of the excitement of seeing the rare sight of a starship, his first, and fatigue from his long journey.

Now, all at once, he had an impression of something alien and silent, all-enveloping. A feeling of isolation came over him, as if the planet were suddenly cut off from the rest of the universe. At the same time, he saw Gullin stiffen, his eyes narrowing. Without needing access to his thoughts, Vidarh knew the other man was feeling something similar.

Before he could react, or analyse the images flitting wraithlike across the periphery of his mind, Tamarith appeared in the hallway. Her face wore an anguished expression and she panted a little from running.

Sorry to interrupt, Gullin...Vidarh, but...I've just had some sort of...some sort of 'vision' I suppose you would call it. There's something...something very strange happening out there, in space. I don't know what it is. I just had a picture in my mind of a barrier in the void...like an invisible wall.

She paused, obviously realising the two men had also experienced something similar. She looked at her brother and then at Vidarh. *I'm going to find out what happened. I will try to contact Jess.*

****

"What now?" Jess ran her fingers over the tactile pads while Dahll studied the data on the main readout screen. "All the propulsion systems have shut down and there's nothing I can do to re-start them.

She addressed the computer. "*Seattle?*" Long ago, she had named it after the Chief of one of the ancient tribes of the Americas of Old Earth. "What's going on?"

I regret the necessity of shutting down the main drive. The forcefield is impenetrable.

"According to this data we'd be blasted to a speck of subatomic matter if we go to manual power and attempt to force our way through it," Dahll stated, confirming what Jess already suspected.

She stood, peering over his shoulder to examine the data on the screen. "But who—or what could be generating such a powerful field? This shows it surrounds the whole planet."

Dahll shook his head. "It would take several power sources to generate a forcefield of such magnitude. The *Quest* would surely have picked up the signature of anything large enough to carry out such an undertaking. It's my guess this was only set up after we arrived on Niflheim, and activated when we left."

"I'm going to fire a small probe. We can't give up, not yet. The computer might be wrong."

"It's not likely, but it's worth a try."

"Fire exploratory probe number three," Jess commanded. The holographic image wore an expression of concern. *Such a procedure is pointless, the probe will be consumed by the energy trans—*

"Don't argue with me, please, just do it!"

A moment later, the probe was fired and at almost the same moment, the computer's prediction confirmed. They both shielded their eyes from the back flash that lit up the screen, while the *Quest* rocked slightly in as if in protest.

"Then...there's nothing we can do." Jess turned to Dahll, unable to conceal her despair. "We've failed them. We can't get the help we need for Niflheim, we can't even leave the planet!"

Dahll put a comforting arm around her shoulders. "We won't give up yet. Why not put the *Quest* into geostationary orbit around the planet and get the computer to examine the available data to see if it can come up with a solution?"

She nodded. They needed to stay positive. "Perhaps if we wait for a while the forcefield will dissipate naturally, after all it wasn't there before—"

"It's possible," Dahll agreed, "although I reckon it's been configured to activate whenever a ship approaches. It's obviously designed to prevent ships leaving Niflheim..."

"Or to keep ships from landing there," Jess suggested. "But it seems a very elaborate course of action considering so few ships visit Niflheim. Whoever—or whatever set it up must have had a pretty good reason for doing it...but what?"

Dahll shook his head slowly. "It looks like that's something we're going to have to find out—and find a solution to, if we're ever to get to Phidia." He paused for a moment. "Shall we give it twenty ship's hours? If the force shield's still there then, I can't see any other option than to return to Gladsheim and tell them what's happened."

Jess frowned. "There's no point in staying here in stationary orbit indefinitely. I hate the thought of failing before we've even begun, though."

After making the necessary adjustments to the controls, she turned to Dahll, still methodically feeding commands into the computer. "While you're trying to find some sort of solution there, I'm going to the Sick Bay to set up some of those tissue samples for analysis with the medical computer. It might not be able to come up with a cure but at least I'll feel we're doing something. It might also help save a bit of time for the Phidians, when we eventually get there."

Dahll looked up briefly. "I just hope we can come up with some answers before it's too late."

****

In the Sick Bay Jess set up the samples and programmed the computer to analyse them, with a view to isolating and identifying the virus. On her return, she found Dahll still poring over the accumulation of data on the screens before him.

He looked up as she approached, and gave her a rather weary smile. "I've still not been able to ascertain the source of the forcefield. If you've finished, we might as well try to get some sleep. There doesn't seem to be very much more we can do for now."

"True. We won't be much good to the Nifls if we're too tired to think straight."

All the same, part of her wanted to stay, to try

to fathom out a resolution to the impasse they had come up against so unexpectedly.

Neither of them could sleep, however, and they soon gave up trying and returned to the Flight Deck. Although they kept themselves busy examining data and calculating the possibilities, they were still no nearer to finding a solution by the end of their self-imposed twenty ship's hours limit. The forcefield stayed stubbornly immovable and intact.

"That's it, then," Jess said without enthusiasm. "We'll just have to return to Niflheim and hope the *Quest's* medical computers can find a remedy."

"You never know," Dahll said, "the forcefield might be a natural phenomenon and could disappear as quickly as it came. We can set up the *Quest's* scanners to alert us if it does."

Jess nodded. "I wonder if it's affected by distance. Shall we move back a few hundred spacials, and see what happens?" She took the controls and with expert precision, moved the small craft out of orbit and back toward the planet. At the appointed distance, Dahll ran a computer scan. The forcefield no longer registered.

"If it were still active the computer would easily pick it up from here," he said, with a thoughtful expression. "Let's try turning her around again, maintaining course at half power."

Jess turned the craft about and reduced the power. At precisely the same point as before, the computer alerted them to the forcefield ahead and shut down the power to the drives. She slowly eased the *Quest* back and set up the co-ordinates for Niflheim.

"Well that proves something at least," she said softly. "We know whatever that forcefield *is* out there, it's capable of registering an oncoming craft and activating itself. Something wants to keep us from leaving Niflheim."

"It certainly looks that way. We've done all we can. I suggest we put the *Quest* on auto-pilot for the return to Niflheim and try to get some rest, now."

Jess set the controls, tension in her shoulders. She was, she had to admit at last, feeling very tired. A short while later she lay, with Dahll's arms wrapped around her, in that state of not being asleep, yet not fully awake, when she heard the 'voice' in her head.

This time she knew it belonged to Tamarith. She heard it clearly now, like the first time Tamarith had spoken to her telepathically, on their very first visit to Niflheim.

Not fully certain what she was doing, she concentrated her thoughts, and cleared her mind of all external influences. Drawing on everything she'd learnt from Gullin and Tamarith, she mentally formed a message so that Tamarith would know they were on their way back to Niflheim.

Chapter Six

When the *Quest* made planetfall on the Drasil Plain once more, the darkness of night covered the landscape. An eerie silence hovered over the surface, beneath the ethereal veil of mist covering the snow-clad land. Jess supposed most of Gladsheim was sleeping.

As on their last visit, they had landed as close to the settlement of Gladsheim as they could without endangering any of the buildings or inhabitants. This meant they could easily make the short journey on foot, without the hover-hopper they normally used as transport over difficult terrain or for travelling long distances.

The single moon showed barely a crescent, so Dahll made use of several light-spheres from the *Quest's* store to illuminate the hull while he set his shielding device.

"Best not to take any chances," he muttered. "Something odd's going on. It's as if something *meant* us to come back here for some reason, and I'd rather not wait until the morning to set this up."

Jess adjusted her wrist flare to a steady beam and shone it on the area where Dahll was working, to supplement the light from the spheres. It took only a few minutes for him to position and calibrate the shield.

"We'd best be going then," she said, as soon as he stepped down, after returning the spheres to the store. "I'm not sure, but I've a feeling we're being watched. Let's hope someone will be awake when we arrive at Gladsheim, else we might have to sleep in

47

the barn with the ponies."

She stopped, her body stiffening, sure they were not alone. She put her hand to the stunner gun at her hip. Jess hated violence and did not expect to find any here, but experience had taught her complacency was dangerous. It was better to be prepared than caught unawares.

"And do you really think we could allow you to do such a thing?"

A figure stepped out from the shadow of one of the tall evergreens that grew in abundance in the more temperate regions of Niflheim.

Dahll put a hand on Jess's shoulder, and she relaxed and replaced the gun in its holster.

"Gullin," Dahll said, how did you know we'd be here?"

"Forgive me, I did not mean to alarm you. I waited for your ship to arrive." He turned to Dahll. "In answer to your question, I have been in touch with Tamarith. My sister's powers of telepathy are advanced, but Jess seems to have latent telepathic abilities, too. Tamarith received her thought waves and knew you were returning. She told me when you were about to arrive, so I waited here for you. I could not let you make your way to Gladsheim alone. That would be unpardonably discourteous."

"We could never think that of any of your family," Jess said, shaking off her embarrassment at having been spooked. "We didn't expect anyone to meet us. We're just sorry we've had to come back without being able to get help for you from Phidia."

"At least you returned safely. We would never have forgiven ourselves if you had been in danger because of us. Tell me, what exactly was it that prevented you from entering deep space?"

"Some sort of forcefield, surrounding the whole planet, according to our sensors. Thankfully our computer detected it well before we were at risk of running into it, and shut down the main drives," Jess told him. "It was something quite unexpected. Obviously, inertia would have kept us moving toward the field, so we went into orbit while we decided what to do, and collected some data on the forcefield. We'd hoped it might be a natural phenomenon that would dissipate, if we waited, but when it showed no signs of doing so, we had no option but to return."

"I reckon it's not been there very long," Dahll put in, as they walked the short distance to the Rainbow Bridge. "It's as if some powerful force constructed it to prevent us from leaving,"

"And it would have to be a *very* powerful force to create something like that. It seems to go right around the planet. Dahll and I ran numerous scans but our computer couldn't find any weakness or flaw anywhere."

"But why do you suppose anyone—or anything— would want to prevent you leaving to get help for our people? Niflheim has always been a neutral planet. We have no enemies. We pose no danger to anyone. We do not even have spacecraft of our own."

Jess sighed. "I know. That's something I've been asking myself. It seems to make no sense."

They crossed the bridge in silence and made their way to Gullin's house. As soon as they were inside, Thamri came to greet them, and although obviously concerned by the reason for their return, she looked pleased to see them again. She gave Jess a warm hug, her welcome to Dahll slightly more restrained.

They followed her into the roomy dining hall where a huge log fire crackled and blazed, sending strange shadows cavorting across the walls.

"How's Freya?" Jess asked, glancing around but seeing no cradle.

"She's fine," Thamri assured her in tones of

amusement. "You've hardly been gone long enough for her to have changed much. She's fast asleep in our room. You can have a peek at her later, if you wish, but first you must eat. We've already had our supper but I expect you're hungry?"

A few minutes later, she set steaming plates of vegetable stew before them, and left them together to enjoy their meal. The great hall seemed even bigger, and very empty, without the presence of the numerous people who had occupied it before Jess and Dahll had left for Phidia.

They both ate enthusiastically. They'd not bothered too much about food while they were trying to work out the nature and origin of the mysterious energy field.

"I wonder if Tamarith will join us later," Jess speculated between steaming mouthfuls.

"It is quite late," Dahll reminded her.

"Of course. I just thought she might have been here when we arrived, since she passed my message on to Gullin."

"You'll see her tomorrow, I'm sure. It looks like we may be here for a while."

Jess continued eating in silence. Despite their conversation in the barn, she feared the distance between her and Tamarith was greater than the few buildings separating Gullin and Thamri's home from the one Tamarith shared with Rhenn and Melind. For the moment, however, she kept her anxieties to herself.

Gullin joined him while they finished dessert. Thamri firmly but politely refused their offer of help to clear away the dishes.

"These few things won't take me any time at all," she assured them. True to her word, in only a short while she returned, accompanied by Vidarh.

"Vidarh will be our guest here for tonight," Gullin said, "since Tamarith has gone back with the group from Midgaard. She wishes to stay with them for a while and catch up with some old friends."

Jess could not help thinking there might have been another reason for Tamarith's departure, once she knew of Jess and Dahll's imminent return

"Good evening," Vidarh said, rather formally, "I'm honoured to meet you once more."

"Hello," Jess replied as she and Dahll stood and politely exchanged the Nifl greeting. "It's good to see you again, although unfortunately our very presence here means we have failed in our promise."

"Not necessarily," Dahll contradicted gently. "There's still a chance our ship's medical computer may be able to come up with something."

"I just hope the sickness doesn't become a pandemic before it can find the cure," Jess said.

"Well the virus does not seem to be spreading as fast as we expected," Gullin stated. "In the meantime, we will make the most of your company. Unfortunately this is Vidarh's last night with us."

Vidarh answered Jess's questioning look with a wry grin. "I'm returning to Sleipnir tomorrow I'll be accused of shirking the work if I don't go back soon. Most of the others who came from Sleipnir have already left."

"Is it far to your home?" Dahll asked. "Jess and I have only really seen the regions around Gladsheim and the Drasil Plain. We've never visited any of the other towns and hamlets."

"It's a fair trek. I've left my pony on the other side of the Gunaran Mountains. I hope he hasn't wandered too far. It's a long way to walk."

"You will need one of ours for the crossing to the mountains, and if your own pony is where you left him, just turn ours loose to find its way home," Gullin said. "All our animals know their way back to the warmth and comfort of Gladsheim. Otherwise, you are welcome to keep it to continue your journey.

51

We could do no less."

****

They awoke next morning to find, when they looked out of the window, snow falling heavily. Since it was only late spring on this part of Niflheim, however, that was hardly an unusual occurrence. The lake shimmered softly, like an opaque, blue-grey scarf, casually thrown down upon the landscape. Its silvery sheen contrasted with the virgin whiteness of the snow, which lay in large drifts, splashed with occasional patches of delicate pink. The trees in the distance below the mountains, and those at the edge of the lake itself, stood completely covered with snow, now. Their feathery branches looked like white eagles' wings, raised to the sky.

The beauty of the planet made Jess catch her breath. She could understand the determination of the ancient pioneers of old Earth to colonise it, despite the somewhat inhospitable conditions.

Gullin and Vidarh stood near the fire, apparently conversing telepathically, when they arrived downstairs. Vidarh was not wearing his customary smile, and when Jess met Gullin's gaze she found a look she had never seen there before. Anxiety filled his eyes—and something else, something that looked like despair.

He ran his hands through his hair and his voice, when he spoke, matched his expression.

"There's bad news, I'm afraid. The party heading for Midgaard was ambushed this morning, just beyond the Gunningap Mountains. They fought hard, but were no match for their attackers. One of our friends was killed. The others have all been taken prisoner—including Tamarith."

Chapter Seven

For a moment, Jess and Dahll stood in silence. Vidarh moved to one side as Jess, clearly shocked, stepped forward and laid a sympathetic hand on Gullin's arm. "Gullin, I am so sorry. When did this happen?"

"Only a few minutes ago. There was a message from Tamarith that they were being attacked and then...nothing."

Thamri, her face pale and with none of her usual cheer, descended the staircase with Freya in her arms. Rhenn and Melind followed close behind. Vidarh could not help noticing how the usually vivacious Melind moved despondently, with her head lowered. A wave of sympathy for the girl, as well as for Thamri, washed over him. His own senses were still numbed by the recent events. The image of Tamarith swam in his mind.

Rhenn, too, looked subdued. "Gullin has told you?" he asked Jess.

"Yes, I'm still struggling to make sense of it." She put her arms around Melind, who looked close to tears.

"Any idea who might have been responsible for this...kidnapping, if that's what it is?" Dahll asked.

Gullin shook his head slowly. "There has never been such an incident on our world before. None of our people would do such a thing—what would be their motive?" He looked at Vidarh, clearly perplexed. "It's not as if we are an economically-based culture. We are farmers and barterers. We have nothing worth holding any of our people to ransom for." He indicated that they should seat themselves in the dining hall. "I will send Liftrar a message and ask him to join us. I know it's hard to think of food at a time like this, but none of us has eaten yet. Perhaps we might be able to think more clearly, after we have breakfasted.

Thamri laid the baby in a cot in the corner where she would feel the warmth from the fire, then bustled about making sure everyone had enough to eat and drink, as if determined not to give herself chance to think.

Vidarh glanced through the windows between mouthfuls, wishing he could will the snow to stop. Less than an hour had passed since Tamarith's anguished thoughts had reached him and Gullin. Frightened, shocked, she had flashed a picture in his mind of blood upon snow, his acquaintance Lars, lying still and lifeless. He 'saw' Tamarith struggling with a tall, shadowy figure. Then silence.

The scene transmitted in his mind had ceased as abruptly as it had started, and he assumed whoever had taken her and her companions had somehow rendered them unconscious. They were still alive, he was sure of it. That did not stop him from worrying and wondering where she was and how she was being treated.

They had almost finished eating when there was a knock on the door.

Liftrar, come in," Gullin said, "The door is not locked." The old man shuffled in, his expression grave. Gullin beckoned him to sit near the fire and everyone pulled up seats close by.

"Never can I recall anything like this happening before, not in all of Niflheim's history. It is a sad day," Liftrar said, rubbing gnarled hands together in front of the fire.

"Whoever did this thing to our friends, and our sister, will pay for it. Even if it takes the rest of my life to find them," Rhenn declared, his young face grim, his eyes glinting.

Dahll leaned forward, frowning. "Gullin, you said earlier it was unlikely anyone from Niflheim would have perpetrated this crime. If it's not your own people who've kidnapped them, it must be outsiders...other-worlders."

Liftrar looked across at him, his lips compressed in a thin line. "But for what purpose?"

A looked passed between Jess and Dahll, and Vidarh wondered if he was the only one who noticed it.

"Has there been any report of a small starship or an unidentified ferry rocket landing here recently?" Jess asked.

Gullin shook his head. "No, but there are many places on Niflheim where a ship could land unnoticed."

Jess looked back at Gullin. "You are able to make mental contact with Tamarith, wherever she is, aren't you? Can't you re-establish the link, find out what's happening?"

"That is the problem," Gullin said, his voice heavy with anxiety. "After the message from her, telling us about the attack and that Lars had been killed and they had been taken prisoner, the connection between us was broken abruptly. I've been trying but I can no longer reach her or any of the others. Vidarh received her message too, and lost contact at the same time I did."

Vidarh nodded. "For some reason we can't re-establish it,"

Thamri sat beside her husband, clasping his arm. "It is traumatic to be cut off from them so suddenly. We all are so used to being able to communicate with each other whenever we are apart. This is especially true of family members. Of course, we tend to have our minds open to each other most of the time." She hesitated, her voice husky with emotion. "Tamarith is my husband's sister. We had grown close. We would know if she...if she were not still alive." She looked at Gullin, as if for assurance.

Reaching across, Gullin took his wife's hand and held it in his. "Just as we knew Lars had lost his life. We all felt it."

"They must have been taken for a purpose," Dahll said. "Presumably they weren't carrying anything of value with them?"

Thamri shook her head wordlessly.

"Then robbery won't have been the motive. Their attackers are unlikely to have harmed them if they've taken them prisoner, and they must still be on this planet. If they'd tried to take off with their captives, they'd have had to neutralize the shield. It's still there. I have a remote communicator set up with the *Quest's* computer, and if the field had deactivated, it would have registered. The *Quest* would also have detected any alien ships attempting to leave Niflheim's atmosphere."

"We will organise some sort of search party, and follow the route they were taking to Midgaard," Gullin stated. "They would not have been able to travel very far yet, and they may have been hampered by the snow." He turned to look behind him, through one of the large windows. "At least this morning's snowfall seems to have blown over. We must hope it is only a spring shower. It might have covered the tracks though."

"We'll help you," Jess said, with a glance at Dahll. "It looks as if we're not going to be able to set out for Phidia for a while, so we'll use the time to try and find Tamarith and the rest of the party."

"You would really help us search for them?"

For the first time that morning, Vidarh observed a glimmer of hope in Gullin's dark eyes.

"Of course," Dahll assured him. "You don't think we could just sit around here when Tamarith and her friends are missing—are in danger?"

"It's almost as if we were meant to stay here and help you try to find them," Jess added.

"I thank you, my friends. But three of us will not be enough. We still do not know what we are up against."

"I'm coming too," Melind said.

"And you, Rhenn?"

The young man shook his head. "Gullin, you're more receptive to Tamarith than any of us. *You* need to go but someone should stay here—we can't all go in case the kidnappers come back this way."

After a slight pause, Gullin nodded. "There is that to be considered and I *would* feel happier if Thamri was not left here alone. I'd ask you to come too, Vidarh, but I know you are leaving for Sleipnir this morning."

Vidarh met Gullin's glance and hesitated, torn between his growing concern over Tamarith and a sense of guilt because he had already been away from his home longer than anticipated.

He felt as if a heavy weight were pressing on him. He'd sat in silence during most of the discussion, the picture of Tamarith's anguished face still in his head as she fought an adversary much larger than herself. One she could not have hoped to overcome. The thought of what she might be enduring tore at his heart.

However, he had a duty to his family, which he could not ignore. "Yes, I ought to be getting back. I should have left already." He tried not to sound disparaging. "My sister and brothers are quite capable of helping my parents run the farmstead, but the ponies are my particular responsibility. I don't want it to look like I'm making excuses not to return."

He smiled apologetically through gritted teeth. Tamarith still lived...he needed to keep hold of that one fact.

"I understand. Your family needs you."

Vidarh thought for a moment, and came to a decision. "I could come with you as far as Midgaard," he said with sudden resolve. "It won't be far out of my way, and I can continue on to Sleipnir from there. I'll contact my family to let them know what's happened and warn them to be watchful for marauders."

"Thank you," Gullin said. "If we are swift, we may catch up with the kidnappers and their prisoners before they reach Midgaard, which seems to be where they're headed. I appreciate your help, all of you."

"Then let's get started," Vidarh said. "Gullin, we'll need ponies, shall I get them ready?"

"Yes, and I'll sort out things here. You will probably find Helva and Narvi in the barn. They will tell you which are the best animals."

"I'll help," Melind said quickly, abruptly breaking the uncharacteristic silence she had kept during their meal. "It'll be quicker with two of us to saddle them."

Before Vidarh could reply, a piercing shriek rent the air, sending demonic echoes reverberating throughout the building.

Then it came again.

Right outside the door.

Chapter Eight

"Malmooth!" Jess exclaimed. "You know, I've never forgotten that sound, or the first time I heard it. I wondered where he was."

"He's been hibernating in the mountain caves," Gullin said. "He may be Tamarith's pet, but he still has the instincts of a wild animal, to sleep over the winter. I knew he would return as soon as she sent us her message about the ambush. It would have reached him, as well."

His brow furrowed, Gullin concentrated on the heavy wooden door, until it ceded to his will and slowly swung open. A large, bear-like creature bounded in and shook itself vigorously. The assembled group stepped back as drops of water from the melted snow flew in all directions from the icecat's creamy-white pelt. Malmooth howled again, not so loudly this time, a sound more resembling a high-pitched whine. He sat down before Gullin, with one paw raised, his head cocked and his huge golden eyes filled with anguish.

Melind ran over and knelt beside him. She stroked him gently, while Gullin, with closed eyes, laid a hand on the animal's head.

"I've sent him soothing vibes and told him to stay here, that we're discussing what to do about Tamarith and the others," he explained after a moment. "It's a pity these creatures can only receive telepathically and are unable to communicate back, but I'm sure he understands that as far as we know Tamarith has not been harmed." Gullin turned back to the icecat, which moved to a part of the room

59

away from the door, then stretched out to his full length, laying his head on his front paws.

"He's magnificent. We have a couple at our farmstead, as guard animals and also for wool, but not like him," Vidarh said in admiration. Then, turning to Melind, he added, "Come, we'd better move if we're going to sort those ponies out."

Melind nodded and followed Vidarh out to the barn, closing the door behind them.

Jess rose to her feet. "We'd better get back to the *Quest* and decide what we need to take with us."

Thamri nodded and went over to the cradle. She picked up the sleeping infant and laid her in Gullin's arms. "I suppose the rest of you will be leaving soon. Spend a little time with your daughter, now. Who knows when you will be back with us again?" Her face wore a wistful expression as she looked into her husband's eyes. "I wish I were coming with you. I should be riding at your side."

"If only it were not necessary to leave you and Freya...but I am closer to Tamarith than even Rhenn and Melind. I will surely be able to sense her if we manage to get near them and their captors. There will not be a moment I am not thinking of you both while we're away, and we'll always be able to touch with our minds."

Dahll looked down at the sleeping child. "She's one of the most contented babies I've ever seen," he said softly, a gentle expression in his eyes. He put his hand on Jess's arm. "You're right, we should be leaving. I don't know how long we'll be, Gullin. We'll check the samples while we're there, to see if the computer's managed to come up with anything yet, but we'll be back as soon as we can."

"While you're gone we'll pack some provisions for the journey. Is there anything else you'll be needing?" Gullin asked.

"Thanks, but I think we'll be able to get

everything we need from the ship," Jess told him. "We've lightweight heat-suits and thermal footwear on board, and apart from a few personal items we won't need much else."

****

The snow lay in drifts of pink and white, unmarked by even the footprints of a small bird or mammal, as if a huge, irregularly chequered blanket had been laid over the land. Vidarh studied the sky. Both suns were clearly visible, the golden G-type's rays warm and reassuring. After the snowfall, the land was clear of the mist, which frequently covered even this oasis in the desert of snow and ice that was Niflheim. With luck, they would be able to commence their journey in clear conditions.

He glanced behind, to see the diminutive Melind struggling almost up to her knees as she tried to keep up with him. He shortened his stride and slowed down enough for her to reach his side. Together they covered the short distance to the barn that housed the ponies. When they reached it, a snowdrift piled high against the door barred their way. They looked at each other for a moment, then applied their telekinetic powers to shift away enough of the snow to enable them to open the door.

The ponies, snug in their stalls, turned as they entered, their breath forming clouds in the cold air, which accompanied Melind and Vidarh through the doorway. Vidarh inhaled the familiar smell of hay and horses and straw damp with fresh droppings.

Dunno where Helva and Narvi are, Melind telepathed, walking to the end of the stable area. She opened another door that led into a room with saddles and bridles neatly arranged on racks on the walls. Each set had a small wooden plaque above it inscribed with the name of the pony it fitted.

There are some more ponies in the pasture by the river. They've probably gone to check on them. We

could ask them to come back, I suppose...d'you think?
She took down a bridle, and shook out the reins
before looping them over her arm, looking up into his
eyes as she asked her question.

He was struck by how much like her sister she
looked, especially now, when her dark eyes wore the
same sad expression that had been in Tamarith's the
last time he'd seen her.

Why did Tamarith keep troubling him so much?
He'd only known her a short while. It wasn't as if
she were the only one the kidnappers had taken. He
was concerned about the others just as
much...wasn't he?

He brought his mind back to the task in hand.

*Not a lot of point in bothering them. We can
manage ourselves, I'm sure. I'm a fair judge of horses
myself,* Vidarh commented.

*And I know the ponies just as well as Helva and
Narvi do. You take Dancer's tack and I'll show you
which is his stall. We'd best get a move on before
Dahll and Jess get back.*

****

As soon as they were outside the door and
headed toward the Rainbow Bridge, Jess turned to
Dahll and voiced the question that had been on her
mind since they had first learnt of the abduction of
Tamarith and her companions.

"If the group heading for Midgaard was not
carrying anything worth being robbed for, and
they're not being held for ransom—"

"There's only one other reason why they would
have been taken," Dahll said, as if reading her
thoughts. The concern in his eyes was enough to
confirm the suspicion that had been steadily growing
in her own mind. "And there's only one race we know
of that would brazenly raid peaceful villagers on an
Earth Colony to take slaves—"

Jess shuddered. "I can't bear to think of

Tamarith having fallen into the hands of a Salmaran."

Once they reached the *Quest,* Jess waited impatiently while Dahll deactivated the anti-intrusion device. Inside, she made straight for the Sick Bay to check on the samples she had set up, while Dahll busied himself gathering the things they would need for their journey.

To her disappointment, the computer had made little progress in finding a cure for the mysterious sickness afflicting parts of Niflheim, but there was a mass of data analysis, which she scanned before beginning to pack a few items of medication that might be useful on the journey, including several small bio regenerators.

The computer spoke softly. *I have developed an antiserum, which may help boost the human body's defences against the pathogen. It is not a cure, nor is it guaranteed to give complete protection, but I have confirmed its safety. I would suggest its use as a precaution for those humans who have not previously been vaccinated against similar diseases.*

Jess paused. "What? Seattle, why didn't you tell me earlier? Let's have an analysis of the antiserum." She scanned the mass of data that appeared on the screen. "That looks fine. How much of this can you produce?"

I have manufactured a sample of the vaccine, enough to treat five adult humans. It is a time-consuming process, and although I can use the existing vaccines in the ship's dispensary as a basis, it is necessary to—

"Spare me the details, please. Just tell me how long it will take to produce enough to vaccinate the community here in Gladsheim."

According to the latest population statistics I hold, I calculate that it will take approximately three ship's hours to produce that amount of serum.

"We need to leave soon, so that we can put in some mileage before it gets dark. We can't wait that long. I suppose we'll just have to make do with what we have for the moment."

I repeat that this is not a cure and may have only limited success in providing protection against the disease.

"It's better than nothing, though." Jess picked up the vials from the dispenser and looked around for anything else they might need, just as Dahll entered the Sick Bay.

"Any progress?" he asked.

"We've a small supply of a formula Seattle says may help to protect us from the disease...although it's not guaranteeing anything."

"That's great—"

"Don't get too excited. We only have a little of the vaccine. It'll take about three hours before it can produce enough to distribute among the Nifls in the area, and it's not the real answer. It's just to give the immune system a boost but it's a start. I've finished here. I just want to pick up a few things and we can get back to Gladsheim."

Entering their cabin, she packed her heat-suit and a few other items of clothing, including a long, white, hooded cloak of soft, synthetic fur. Carefully she folded it into a small, neat bundle and slipped it on top of the other things in her travel pack.

"I've kept things to a minimum...don't want to overload the ponies," Jess said, ignoring Dahll's disbelieving grin.

Good thing Dancer's so strong," he kidded as he once more sealed the *Quest* and activated the shield.

He seated himself beside her in the hopper, and as they moved away, Jess looked over her shoulder at the *Quest*, wondering how long it would be before they saw their little ship again.

Chapter Nine

Melind and Vidarh, leading the ponies from the barn, looked up at the approaching vehicle. Thamri, Gullin and Vidarh emerged from the house as the hopper hovered above the ground, then landed and came to a gentle halt. Jess climbed out, closely followed by Dahll.

As Dahll removed their travel packs from the back of the small vehicle, Vidarh watched Jess carefully withdraw five vials from her pocket.

"Our computer's come up with something that may help protect you from the virus, to some degree, although it's not a cure," she told Gullin. "Unfortunately, it could only manage five doses immediately, but it should be able to produce more in a few hours." She took something else from her pack. "This is an auto-hype, very easy to use, and quite painless," she explained, as Vidarh, unable to hide his curiosity, studied the objects she held.

"Rather than all of us hanging around until the rest of the doses are produced," Dahll said, "Perhaps someone else could fetch them from our ship when they're ready?"

Jess touched his arm, looking up at him. "Except it's not going to be that easy for anyone not familiar with it to disarm the ship's anti intrusion device. Why don't we let Gullin and the others go on ahead with the ponies, and wait here ourselves, until the rest of the antiserum is ready? We can fetch it from the *Quest* in the hopper and then catch up."

A figure emerged from the shadows. Vidarh recognised Hermot, the physician who had brought the tissue samples for Jess and Dahll to take to Phidia.

"I think perhaps you'd better show me how this works," he stated, "seeing that it's in advance of anything we have on Niflheim. I need to be able to use it myself, so I can vaccinate the others when we get more supplies."

Vidarh watched the procedure with interest and was surprised at how painless the process was when it came to his turn.

Within a short space of time the necessary vaccinations had been carried out, and Gullin's party prepared to leave.

Gullin put his arms around his wife and child, then held out his hand, first to Dahll, then to Jess, not in the Nifl fashion, but clasping their hands in a firm handshake.

"We'll see you sometime tomorrow," he said, and climbed into his saddle.

They moved off at a swift lope. As he rode, Vidarh concentrated all his efforts on projecting a message to Tamarith. He tried not to speculate on what might happen to her if they were unable to find her and the other captives.

****

When Jess and Dahll arrived back at their ship they went straight to the Sick Bay.

"Have you completed the batches, Seattle?"

Affirmative, the computer responded. *There are currently one thousand, five hundred doses available for use.*

Jess turned to Dahll. "Is that going to be enough?"

"Seattle thinks it is. I'm not quite sure how many there are at Gladsheim at the moment, but the computer must have reasonably accurate information in its data banks. There should be enough to go around, at least until we get back and can collect some more."

Swiftly they packed the vials of antiserum into lightweight containers and loaded them into the hopper.

"I suppose the barrier is still in place," Jess said, "or Seattle would have registered a change. Better check though...*Seattle*, what's the position with regard to the forcefield around this planet. Is there any change?"

Negative, the computer intoned, with what sounded like a trace of annoyance. *The forcefield remains in place. I will inform you if the situation changes.*

Dahll took a final look around. "Let's be off while we still have an hour or so of daylight left."

Once back at the settlement, they deposited the precious vials of serum with Hermot, keeping back a small supply to take with them.

Thamri would not let them leave before sitting down to steaming mugs of soup to set them up for their journey. As soon as they could, they thanked her and said their goodbyes.

Jess called Malmooth to follow them to the hopper. The ice cat with its keen sense of smell and telepathic empathy with Tamarith, might prove useful.

He seemed to understand when Jess pointed to the vehicle, and clambered into the back. This time Dahll took the controls, and Jess turned and waved until she could no longer see Thamri or even the buildings. She then hunkered down and concentrated on the landscape before them.

In order to save power, Dahll did not push the vehicle too hard. The party on horseback would not travel much more than twenty-five kilometres. They would need to ride to the end of the Gunaran range and back over the Drasil Plain, skirting the mountains down to the Gunningap Pass, since they could not take the ponies through the caves. It would not take the hopper long to catch up.

The hoof prints were clearly visible in the layer of fresh snow from the morning's fall. Jess still found the areas of pink snow fascinating, a result, Tamarith had once told her, of minute plant forms that dispersed themselves with the snow and would take root as soon as the weather was warm enough.

They skimmed the base of the Gunaran Mountains and the forest on the other side. The vegetation grew more and more sparse. Eventually it petered out altogether, and gave way to the vast Drasil Plain.

To the east, as far as they could see, lay nothing but snow and ice, barren land, seeming almost as desolate and inhospitable as the wastelands beyond Angrboda, of which Gullin had spoken.

They were about to turn westward, toward the Brynhild Peaks, and the narrow Gunningap Pass, when the mist, so prevalent on Niflheim, descended, without any warning. Even the powerful light of the hopper could not pierce the murky greyness and with some reluctance, Dahll brought the vehicle to a halt. He turned and gave Jess one of his slow smiles, with a little gesture of resignation. "It looks as if that's as far as we're going to be able to go today."

Jess nodded. "We don't know if there are glaciers ahead or what other dangers we might run into."

"We're certainly better off here in the open than going near those mountains and risking getting caught in an avalanche."

It did not take long to erect their small but serviceable portable shelter, while Malmooth went off to forage. Once they had the light globes working and the integral heating unit fired up, their temporary quarters were almost as comfortable as any permanent structure. They soon had a hot meal prepared from the provisions Thamri had given them.

After their meal, Jess spread out their heated sleeping bag and snuggled into the soft bedding, which immediately conformed to her shape. A few moments later Dahll joined her, wrapping his arms around her and kissing her hair, before moving down to her lips.

"What's on your mind, Jess?"

"What makes you think anything is?" she asked, slipping an arm around his neck.

"You've not been quite your usual self all day."

"Am I that transparent?"

"Only to me. What's worrying you?"

"Nothing, really. Just thinking."

Dahll drew her close. "Come on Jess, I know you better than that. Tell me, please."

"I'm worried about Tamarith and the others. There's an awful lot of land out there. Land we don't know. Suppose we don't find them until it's too late? What if the Salmarans get them back to their ship before we find them?"

"Hey, we don't know for sure who's taken them and if they even have a ferry down here. If it *is* the Salmarans, they might be waiting for a ferry to land on a given signal. And we may not know the terrain, but Gullin and the others do. It's not like you to be negative."

"I can't help wondering who's behind the forcefield and why they're stopping us from leaving. It's not only that, though. I'm not sure why, I just have a feeling there's something else. Something I can't quite put my finger on."

****

They woke shortly after daybreak, and, disentangling herself from Dahll's embrace, Jess rose and peered through the window of their shelter. The sunlight streamed through.

They prepared their morning meal before packing away their bedding and dismantling the shelter. When they had stashed it in the back of the hopper, they called for Malmooth and all climbed aboard. They travelled a few kilometres, and were close to the narrow pass, when Jess, who was at the controls, looked across at the mountains thoughtfully.

"I think we should skirt the Brynhild Peaks, rather than go through the Gunningap Pass," she mused. "If we cut across the Drasil Plain we can hit the trail again ahead of Gullin's party, and wait for them. It'll be easier than taking the hopper between the mountains."

Dahll looked at her enquiringly. "I reckon there's more to your reasoning?"

She shrugged. "I'm not sure. I just have a feeling...trust me, Dahll, it won't do any harm to take the easier route."

"We can't afford to waste power, though," he warned as she eased the vehicle along the base of the mountains. "I checked the solar cells earlier and they're not going to last much longer than another eight hours or so, even if we manage to absorb some sunlight now."

"It's not as if we're going out of our way," Jess replied. "And—Dahll!"

She brought the hopper to an abrupt halt. Lying in the snow, tinted crimson with their own blood, lay two motionless bodies.

Chapter Ten

The darkness lay around her like a shroud. Tamarith struggled to sit up. Panic welled in her. She tried to control her trembling, not from the cold, for her warm icecat wool coat kept out the worst of the chill, but from her inherent fear of the dark. How many times had she woken up like this in the dark? Where was she? How did she get here?

She gritted her teeth, taking deep breaths. She sensed others lying on the ground nearby, but although she sent out waves of thought, she could reach no other mind and discerned they were still unconscious.

She eased her stiff limbs into a more comfortable position and struggled to draw together the tattered remnants of her mind. The ground beneath her was hard, and slippery with moisture. The dank, frigid air smelt like rotting fungi. Loneliness threatened to overwhelm her. It took every ounce of her willpower to force herself to think logically, to close her eyes against the all-enveloping blackness and try to find a way to help herself and her companions.

Tamarith tried to send out another message. Surely Gullin would come after her? Eventually, having tried unsuccessfully for several minutes, she decided she would have to conserve her energy and try again later. Why could she not reach him?

She had to be strong. She could not give up.

She knew she was underground, in some kind of cave complex. There was no sound save that of water dripping from the roof.

Her stomach growled with hunger. Where were her captors? She had become used to losing consciousness and then having them bring food as soon as she woke up. They seemed keen to feed their prisoners regularly, even if they did not seem particularly bothered about their other comforts.

Of course...the food! The realisation hit her like a lightning strike. Why had she not realized it before...the food must be drugged to keep her and her companions from telepathing for help. That was why she could not reach her brother. Whatever was in their rations must be suppressing their telepathic abilities.

She had obviously been unconscious almost continuously since her capture, for she could remember very little since the attack on the way to Midgaard, except that she had managed to transmit a message to Gullin and Vidarh.

Vidarh...he been the first to receive her message, a few moments before Gullin even. Why? What was so special about him? She frowned. Why should there be *anything* special about him? He had been staying with Gullin as his guest, and it was on Gullin she had concentrated her thoughts.

Vidarh had obviously picked up on them because of his physical proximity to her brother.

Opening her eyes once more, she looked around, trying to find some source of light as a relief from the murky blackness. She would not allow herself to believe there was any more to Vidarh's connection with her than that. In fact, she had noticed the covert glances cast in his direction by Melind, and there was a distinct possibility he was more interested in her younger sister. So any sort of attraction beyond their mutual telepathic abilities was the least of her concerns.

She forced herself to concentrate on the darkness around her. As her eyes grew accustomed to it, she realized the gloom was not as complete as she had first thought. The faintest glimmer of light came from somewhere in the distance, but not enough for her to be able to make out her surroundings.

There was also something in front of her, something intangible, sensed rather than seen, although tiny sparks of invisible light seemed to emanate from it into her mind. She stretched out a cautious hand, to withdraw it immediately with a sharp cry as something like an electric shock ran through her.

A forcefield...it had to be. She vaguely remembered Dahll mentioning something about forcefields on his first visit to Niflheim, when he had been discussing protecting The *Quest*.

Tamarith shrank back against the solid, damp walls of her prison as she heard voices and a bright light suddenly illuminated the caves. She remembered the hunger gnawing at her stomach and realized their captors must be returning at last, to bring them food. She did not have much time. She closed her eyes again, and concentrated all her energy on trying once more to transmit a message.

*****

Jess, closely followed by Dahll, leapt out of the hopper and knelt beside the prone bodies almost before the vehicle had halted. Malmooth followed, sniffed both of the still forms curiously, then backed off and sat still. Raising his head to the skies, he howled once—an unearthly, mournful cry that cut into the still air, then ran around in circles muzzle to the ground, as if trying to pick up a scent.

The young man and woman sprawled in the snow, some distance from each other, were obviously victims of blaster fire. In the distance, a small herd of ponies shovelled the snow with their muzzles to get at the young grass beneath.

Dahll knelt by one of the shattered bodies in the blood-soaked snow. "Helva and Narvi," he said softly. "I'm afraid Narvi's dead, and has been for a while."

"Helva?" With gentle hands, Jess touched Helva's forehead, and realized she was still, somehow, clinging to life. She wore a hooded coat of leather, thickly lined with icecat wool, with several more layers underneath. The toughness of her outer garment was obviously the only reason she had not been killed instantly. Its warmth had prevented her from succumbing to hypothermia, although Jess hated to think how many hours she might have been lying there. The wound was grave, and blood trickled from the corner of her mouth. Plainly she did not have long to live.

"I...I'm sorry—" she started, then coughed and gasped for breath.

"Hush, Helva, don't try to talk." Jess looked up at Dahll, wondering what the girl meant. Dahll had one of the *Quest's* small bio-regenerators in his hand but obviously realized the damage was too extensive for it to be effective. Instead, he administered a swift-acting analgesic.

Jess flicked a ghost of a smile at him. At least they could relieve her pain if they could not save her life.

The girl's eyes fluttered open, and as she saw the fear in them, Jess felt tears of compassion well in her own.

"I...I need...to...tell you..."

Jess took hold of Helva's hand. "Try to save your energy. The painkiller Dahll gave you should work very soon."

"No...no, I...I must tell you—"

Again, a bout of coughing interrupted her words, bringing up more blood. Jess was amazed the girl could speak at all. She must have been a fair distance from her attacker when they'd shot her, or the blast would have ripped her apart, as it had Narvi.

After she recovered and Jess gently wiped the blood from her face, Helva said, "We...we'd been rounding up the ponies...they'd strayed from the pastureland. Then...then we saw the...strangers. They...they were not of this world." She paused, her breath coming in little gasps and wheezes.

Dahll and Jess exchanged glances.

"They...they promised to pay us well if...if we helped them...but...they never intended to pay us...they...they..."

Her words faded away and Jess, aching with sadness and a deep disappointment, placed the hand she had been holding across Helva's blood-soaked breast.

"She's gone," Jess murmured, biting her lip, her eyes moist. "She was so young."

Dahll nodded and put his arm around her shoulder. "Such a waste. I wonder what she was trying to tell us. Sounds like they betrayed their own people."

"I suppose the temptation was too much," she said on a jagged breath, struggling for composure. Do you think it was the Salmarans?"

Dahll shrugged. "Hard to say."

"We can't just leave them."

"We have the hopper. The sonic cutters are in there, they'll cut through the ground, however hard it is underneath the snow. We can at least give them the dignity of a burial."

Jess followed him to the hopper. The sonic cutters made short work of digging the graves. When they had buried the two young Nifls, Dahll stood solemnly while Jess knelt and said a prayer, staying with her head bowed for a moment, before rising to her feet. "I don't know if they worshipped the

Universal Spirit," she said, "but I thought someone should speak and ask forgiveness on their behalf."

Dahll nodded. "Ever a missionary, eh, sweet? Do you miss your old vocation?"

"Only at times like this," she answered, her voice serious. "But I wouldn't want to change anything now. I can't imagine a life without you."

Without speaking, he put his arm about her. They walked back to the hopper and called to Malmooth, who stood, his nose pointed toward Midgaard, as if to confirm the direction taken by the killers. Taking one last look at the two small mounds, they seated themselves in the vehicle and headed for the Brynhild Peaks.

Hovering a short distance above the ground, they passed along the foot of the mountain range and headed west. They made for an area of woodland beside the rough track leading to Midgaard, where a shallow stream trickled down from the mountains. Jess looked at the power gauge of the small vehicle.

"That's pretty much it, until the cells recharge." She guided the hopper to the edge of the trees and brought the vehicle to a halt. "I think we'd better wait here for the others."

Dahll jumped down and looked at the snow-covered ground. "Well, there aren't any hoof prints so we're ahead of them. We might as well have something to eat while we wait."

They sorted out their food packs, and Malmooth loped off to the tree line where he began to browse on the lower branches, uttering little grunts of appreciation.

"Best not light a fire," Jess said, settling herself at the foot of a tree and stretching out her long legs. "We don't want the smoke to be seen."

Dahll sat beside her. "We don't need one anyway. These self-heating packs will be fine. There's some good bread and cheese that Thamri gave us, and it's a fine afternoon." He frowned. "This morning, when you suggested we go past the Brynhild Peaks instead of following the track through the pass, it almost seemed as if you knew we'd find Helva and Narvi" His eyes met hers questioningly.

Jess shrugged. "I just had this strange feeling something was wrong and we needed to go that way. Besides, it made sense to be able to take a short cut and wait for the others, rather than just follow their trail."

She searched her mind for a better explanation but could think of no other answer than a 'premonition'.

After they had eaten, they cut several branches and laid them over the hopper until it was well hidden. Snuggled under the trees, it would not be noticeable from a distance. Dahll also attached a smaller version of the anti-intrusion device he used on the *Quest*.

The suns slipped over the horizon, and a light breeze blew up. The sky darkened in shades of vermillion and purple. The low cloud, swirling down in eddies of drifting mist, hid the tops of the distant mountains and the twilight glowed with an eerie half-light. All at once, Malmooth gave a loud bellow and set off down the track. They could just see several indistinct shapes in the distance, but coming closer.

"I hope it's Gullin and the others," Dahll said, reaching for his blaster. "If it isn't, we'd better be prepared."

Jess was already at his side, her hand hovering over her own weapon. "Malmooth thinks it's them," she said softly, "and I don't think he's wrong."

The riders drew closer, indeed revealing themselves as Gullin and his party.

Holstering their guns, they ran forward to hold

the heads of the ponies as Gullin and Melind dismounted. Gullin bent to pet Malmooth, who was leaping and prancing around like an excited dog.

"How was the journey?" Dahll asked, "Did you see anyone...anything unusual?"

Gullin shook his head. "No, the journey has been uneventful." He turned as Vidarh arrived with the string of spare ponies.

"Hello there," the young man said, vaulting out of the saddle as if it were the start of the day, rather than the end. "It's good to you again, Dahll, Jess. We expected you to catch up with us, not be waiting for us."

"Well, that was Jess's idea, and rather a good one as it happens."

"You must be hungry," Jess said. "We've plenty of food left. There are ample supplies in the hopper and Thamri seems to have packed enough to keep us going for a week."

Vidarh, Gullin and Melind unsaddled their ponies, gave them water and hobbled them, so they could wander and graze the grass among the trees. Then the travellers gathered around the little heating unit from the hopper, to eat the vegetable pies Thamri had made, together with goats' cheese and bread, and fresh fruit.

"I could go to sleep here and now," Melind commented contentedly. "I hadn't realized how hungry I was, but I couldn't eat another thing." She rested her gaze on Vidarh, as she held up a steaming jug of *kobah,* which Jess said reminded her of Terran coffee. "More, anyone?"

"Don't mind if I do," Vidarh said, reaching across so she could refill his mug.

Gullin looked across at his younger sister and although he said nothing and his thoughts were hidden, his expression was stern. To Vidarh, her brother seemed almost disapproving.

****

"I'm afraid we have some bad news," Jess said. She paused, as all eyes turned to look at her. "We found Helva and Narvi this morning, near the Brynhild Peaks. They'd been shot. There was nothing we could do...Narvi was already dead and Helva was barely alive. I'm so sorry."

For a moment, there was stunned silence. Vidarh looked across at Melind and saw her expression had changed from the carefree one she had worn only minutes ago, to a look of stunned disbelief. Seconds later, she seemed close to tears.

Jess walked over and put her arm around the girl. "I'm sorry," she said. "There was no easy way to tell you."

Gullin looked at Jess with narrowed eyes. "Shot, you said?"

Jess nodded. "Yes, they were blaster wounds. Nothing else causes that sort of damage."

"Then it wasn't any of our people."

Dahll shook his head. "Helva was able to speak a little before she died. Their killers were not from Niflheim."

"She said something else, too. We're not sure what she meant," Jess went on. "Something about being sorry. It seems their murderers must have promised to pay them for information—"

"What sort of information could that have been?" Gullin interrupted in disbelief.

Vidarh kept his voice low. "Whoever the killers were...if they're the same people who've kidnapped Tamarith and the others, isn't it likely they'd have tried to find out if anyone was coming after them?

"Or where the nearest settlement is," Dahll offered.

"If that's true," Vidarh said gravely, "Then Midgaard is in danger."

Chapter Eleven

Vidarh was aware of a tightening in his chest and dryness in his throat as he realized that if Midgaard were attacked, Sleipnir would probably be the next target. His main worry though was Tamarith. Neither he nor any of the others had managed to make contact with her and he could not rid himself of the fear something terrible must have happened if she could not receive their messages. She might even have fallen victim to the sickness.

He saw Jess glance at Dahll, who returned her look with a slight nod of his head.

"We think," Jess said gently, "we know who the kidnappers might be...or at any rate where they originate from. Only one species we know has a habit of kidnapping others to sell them as slaves, and that's the Salmarans."

"The same race as the slaver who was after you and Dahll when you first visited Niflheim?" Gullin asked.

Dahll nodded. "We could be wrong, of course, but if it *is* Salmarans we're dealing with, at least we know we're not up against too many of them. Salmaran slavers tend to work alone, with just enough crew to man their ships and overcome their victims." He paused, as if to give emphasis to his words, "And they'll kill anyone else, even their own kind, who tries to trespass on what they regard as 'their' territory. Without knowing for sure, I think our immediate priority must be to contact the residents of Midgaard and warn them to get as many of their people together as possible to prepare for an imminent attack."

Gullin set his mouth in a firm line. "I will contact them tonight. We'd better telepath a message to Gladsheim, also. If we're right about these...abductors, and they landed a ferry rocket in the wastelands—they were obviously making their way south. Gladsheim would logically have been their next target. He paused and looked from Dahll to Jess, then back to Dahll again. "However, in view of where you found Helva and Narvi, it would appear they changed direction and are now moving westward, toward Midgaard. I believe it would still be wise to warn Gladsheim."

"If they were still headed for Gladsheim," Vidarh said, "they would have needed to either double back for several kilometres, or cross the Gunnaran Mountains. It's more logical for them to head west, where there are more settlements."

"Also," Melind added, "it's hard enough to think of Helva and Narvi being traitors. I can't believe they'd tell them about Gladsheim and put their own families in danger."

"You say their killers promised to pay them, and then shot them?" Vidarh asked, turning his attention back to Jess and Dahll.

"That's one of the things that make us believe it's the work of Salmarans," Jess said in a sombre voice. "Once they had all the information they could get, after promising to pay them well, they would have preferred to kill their informants rather than pay up, although I'm surprised they didn't just take them as slaves."

Dahll nodded again. "From the way their bodies were lying, and the fact they'd been shot in the back, they probably tried to make a run for it when they realized the Salmarans' intentions." He paused. "Of course we still can't be certain it's Salmarans, but it's the way they operate. Greed seems to be their main motivation for everything."

"I know you're worried about Thamri and Freya, Gullin," Vidarh said, "but it does look as if Gladsheim is unlikely to be attacked, for the moment, anyway."

"I'll make contact with Thamri. If she's worried or senses any threat to Gladsheim, I'll go back alone." Gullin silenced Vidarh and Melind's protests with a wave of his hand. "No, we cannot afford for more than one to go. It is unfortunate since I am probably the one with the best chance of receiving any communication from Tamarith, but there is no help for it. I have to be with Thamri and Freya if they are in danger."

Vidarh nodded and rose to his feet. "I understand. I'd better check on the ponies now, before we bed down for the night."

Melind leapt up. "I'll come with you. I thought Melody felt a bit lame this afternoon. I'd best check her out."

****

Jess did her best not to look intrigued, as Gullin narrowed his eyes.

"She looked fine to me," he called out after his sister. His critical gaze followed her as she disappeared into the trees, close behind Vidarh, before he turned back to Jess and Dahll. "She is so immature and headstrong, but thinks she is too old to be guided by her elder brother."

"It's not really any of our business," Jess said, "although I somehow get the feeling you don't approve of Vidarh."

"It is this infatuation Melind seems to have for him I don't approve of. She is not being very subtle about it. He's a fine young man, but he must be about ten Terran years her senior. I would not want to see her get hurt. She should be making friends with boys her own age."

Jess gave him an understanding smile. "You can't really blame her for being attracted to Vidarh. He's charming and good-looking. I expect she's flattered he seems to like her company. I wouldn't worry, Gullin, I'm sure you can trust Vidarh not to lead her on."

Gullin's answering smile looked genuine. "I suppose I am being over-protective." He gave Dahll something that looked suspiciously like a wink. "I seem to remember feeling a similar concern for Tamarith five or six years ago, although the circumstances were different and she wasn't hankering after someone so many years older."

"I reckon it's only natural to want to protect the ones we love," Dahll said with an affectionate glance in Jess's direction, "even when they are perfectly capable of looking out for themselves."

****

Slow down Vidarh, can't you?

Vidarh stopped and waited for Melind, panting a little, to catch up with him.

It's really dark now. I can hardly see the ponies under those trees. She adjusted the wrist flare, which Dahll had given her and each of the party, from the *Quest's* reserves. Vidarh watched her unobtrusively by the light from his own flare.

That's better, she telepathed, *I can see the ponies more clearly now.*

Yes. They're all there and quite contented. There's plenty of vegetation for them under the trees and they can drink from the stream. I just wanted to make sure they were all right.

There was a silence, during which Vidarh wondered why Melind had sought him out. Perhaps she was worried about Tamarith and wanted someone to talk with. It had not escaped his notice there was a certain tension between her and Gullin.

Hardly surprising. Gullin had a wife and child

to worry about, as well as Tamarith. He must be under considerable strain.

He wished Melind would relax her mind a little, open up to him. He could sense nothing from her. The ability all telepaths had to close their minds as easily as they could cease speaking aloud, was both a blessing and an inconvenience. He had no wish to intrude on her privacy but he could not help wondering why she was being so careful to shield her thoughts if she needed to confide in him. Not that he could offer much reassurance when he was so fearful for Tamarith's safety himself.

Try not to worry about Tamarith and her friends. I'm sure we'd know if anything had happened to them.

Melind slipped a halter over her mare's head. *I know. I just hope we pick up the trail soon so we can make a rescue plan. Can you give me a hand with Melody?*

Of course. You said she was lame?

Umm, no, not exactly. She just felt a bit...oh I don't know, a bit stiff somehow.

Vidarh ran his hand down the mare's leg while Melind held her. *The leg feels cool enough. She should be fine by morning. Feel for yourself.*

He held the mare's head while Melind ran her own hand down the pony's foreleg, and, lifting up the hoof, inspected it closely with her wrist flare, before carefully scraping away the compacted snow with the small pick she carried in her belt.

Yes. Seems all right. Perhaps she stepped on a stone and made it sore for a while. She released the hoof and turned back to Vidarh. *Thanks, you can let her go now.*

Vidarh slipped off the animal's halter and allowed her to rejoin the other ponies before he turned to the girl. *Are you sure there's nothing else worrying you, nothing you want to talk about?*

Of course not. Why d'you say that?

I think we both know there wasn't really anything wrong with Melody, so I assumed you wanted to talk to me about something.

By the light of his flare, Vidarh saw a flush spread over Melind's pretty features. When she lowered her eyes, he was even more convinced she was hiding something.

With a sudden flash of comprehension, he chided himself for his naivety. He had lived long enough, and been around enough young girls, to realize she had a crush on him.

He would need to tread carefully to make sure he didn't hurt her.

****

When they emerged from their various shelters the next morning, more snow had fallen, and now a low mist lay over everything, turning the trees to phantoms, and casting a spectral silence over the landscape. Distances distorted and landmarks that stood out the night before had either disappeared or mysteriously changed shape.

An appetising, spicy smell wafted toward Vidarh from the pot of fruit and oatmeal bubbling over the heating unit.

"Morning everyone. Did you contact Thamri?" he asked Gullin, as they sat down to a hasty but warming breakfast.

Gullin looked more relaxed than he had on the previous evening. "Yes. Thankfully, everything is fine, she says, and she sends greetings to everyone."

Vidarh was secretly relieved. It would have been a difficult situation if Gladsheim were threatened and Gullin felt he had to return. The way ahead was dangerous and even with the five of them, they were likely to find themselves outnumbered.

"Unfortunately," Gullin went on, "I was unable to contact anyone in Midgaard. Melind and I tried

85

together, but we could sense no vestige of life there. At this distance we should have been able to contact them easily, I fear we are too late and they have already been taken."

Vidarh bowed his head for a moment. He had also tried to contact the settlement and hoped Gullin had been more successful.

As soon as their meal was over, he walked over to the ponies with Jess. She took Dancer's halter, and after much patting and words of affection, saddled him and Comet and led them to the hopper. While she unloaded the items she and Dahll had brought with them, and distributed them between the ponies, Vidarh saddled the rest. He had already loaded most of the food packs onto the spare animals.

Jess had told him she had packed a small purifying unit as a precaution, so they could obtain all the water they needed for themselves and the ponies from the icicles in the trees or hanging from the rocks. They could always melt snow as well, if they needed to, so at least they didn't have to worry about giving the ponies the extra burden of carrying water bags.

Once the ponies were ready, Vidarh walked over to where Dahll stood, handing out the blasters brought from the *Quest*.

"You just aim and fire. There are several settings, from 'stun' to 'kill'-—"

Dahll turned as Vidarh approached, and passed one of the weapons to him. Vidarh weighed it experimentally in his hand, then examined the controls set into the butt. He squinted along the sights and Dahll gave him a look of approval.

"You seem at home with that, are you sure you've never handled a blaster before?"

Vidarh shook his head. "Not a blaster, but I've used basic weapons before. It doesn't do to be caught in the mountains around Sleipnir unarmed."

Dahll nodded, and disappeared into the hopper, to re-emerge with a small contraption, which he attached to the side of the vehicle.

"It's a similar unit to the one I use on the *Quest*," he said when Vidarh gave him a questioning look. "It should be enough to prevent any intruders from gaining access to the vehicle, and by keeping the hopper in the open, the solar panels will absorb enough sunlight for it to be fully charged by the time we get back."

Vidarh vaulted onto his pony's back and waited while the others mounted. Once the mist had burnt off and they could see clearly where they were going, they urged the ponies into an easy gallop over the snowy ground.

They made good headway and reached the main trail to Midgaard shortly before midday. Vidarh reined in his mount and the rest of the company pulled up behind him. "I think we should rest the ponies for a spell," he said, "and take a short break ourselves, to eat."

He dismounted and loosened his pony's cinch, then slackened off the pack of the one he had been leading. Removing the bridles, he tied the ropes of the halters they wore underneath to a nearby tree. There was plenty of grass to keep the animals happy while they ate their own meal, and the snow would provide enough moisture to quench their thirst.

The nearer they drew to Nidhogg's Teeth, which lay beyond the settlement of Midgaard, the more his feelings became confused. He was desperately hoping they would find Tamarith and her friends, and overthrow their abductors before they reached the treacherous mountains. He was worried about how the kidnappers were treating Gullin's sister. She had looked so slight and vulnerable the last time he had seen her.

At the same time, although he had not been looking forward to returning to Sleipnir, he was aware the settlement might well be a target for the kidnappers. If they were attacked, would his family survive? Part of him was anxious to return home, to help his family, while his heart urged him to keep searching for Tamarith.

He could at least warn them again. He was about to concentrate his mind on telepathing a message when he was interrupted by the sound of Malmooth's eerie howl. At the same instant, he felt another mind touch his own, and his heart raced uncomfortably. He stood motionless, scarcely believing what was happening. He had not even consciously tried to contact Tamarith, yet somehow she managed to reach him.

Tamarith—have they hurt you?

No, I'm not injured. Vidarh, I was trying to reach Gullin—is he with you, I can't...I can't seem to contact him.

Vidarh had a momentary stab of disappointment that it was apparently Gullin, not himself, Tamarith wanted to speak with. He hastily blotted out the thought. Of course she wanted Gullin, he was her brother. The main thing was that she had made contact. At least he could reassure her they were searching for her. *Tamarith, we're coming to find you. That is Gullin, Melind and myself. Jess and Dahll are with us too...and Malmooth.*

He paused, and looked around at the others, wondering if they too were in contact with Tamarith. They watched him with curiosity etched on their faces.

A wave of immense relief from Tamarith flooded into his mind, telling him she must have been close to despair.

Do you know where you are? Can you give me some way of finding you?

I...I'm not sure. When we walked, we were blindfolded, and when they transported us in the alien vehicle, we were kept unconscious, but I know we're being held in caves somewhere in the mountains. From snatches of conversation I overheard, I'm almost sure they're the ones on the far side of the last range of Nidhogg's Teeth.

What else can you tell me, is there anything that might help us rescue you...and how many others are there?

Swiftly she projected images of her prison, and a mass of information regarding the events since her capture. He sensed she was weakening though, and there was an edge of fear to her thoughts, which she was obviously doing her best to suppress. The news was not good and he drew in a deep breath, trying not to convey his feelings of dismay to her.

I hear Hedrohan coming back. Something must have delayed her for her to stay away so long. We're drugged to keep us from communicating...she doesn't normally allow any of us to come around, other than to eat. I'll pretend to still be unconscious but I won't be able to fool her for long.

Vidarh tried to project a sense of calm and reassurance as she faltered for a moment.

I don't know when...or if I'll be able to reach you again. Be careful...all of you.

As the link was broken, a heavy feeling of loss descended over him, coupled with concern, bordering on fear for the safety of his family and friends.

From what Tamarith had told him, it seemed the slavers' next target would, indeed, be Sleipnir.

Chapter Twelve

"I just had a message from Tamarith, I know where she is," Vidarh said, in answer to the curious stares of the others.

Melind ran up to him, stopping in front of him, her face flushed, and in her excitement forgetting they were in the company of non-telepaths.

What! Where is she? Is she with the rest? How is she...is everyone else all right? How come only you heard her?

Vidarh held up his hands. "Steady on there, Melind, one question at a time. First, yes, as far as I can gather she and the rest are unharmed. They appear to have been rendered unconscious for most of the time. She thinks their food was drugged. She is weak and I was the only one she could reach. I told her we're tracking them." He looked at Gullin, feeling almost apologetic. "I don't know why I was the only one she was able to contact, although Malmooth also picked up something, by the way he's reacting."

Everyone looked at the icecat, which prowled up and down a short distance away, as if behind invisible bars.

Gullin's face showed his relief. "I felt her in my mind, but faintly. At least they are all right, and we know why they have not been able to contact us. But you said you knew where they were?"

"From what I could pick up from Tamarith, I think they're held in the Nidhogg's Teeth range, some distance from Loki's Chasm. It's not just the party from Midgaard who are being held, apparently there are also captives from scattered hamlets and homesteads. She was able to make a brief contact with the prisoners on the ferry, and from what she could pick up from them, it seems the few settlements on the Northern continent were the first to be attacked. Some inhabitants there had already died from the sickness, but those who'd survived were taken and loaded up. The ferry must have then crossed the Burian Sea and landed on the Muspell coast."

"And Midgaard?" Gullin asked, although Vidarh suspected he already knew the answer.

"As we feared, Midgaard itself has already been overcome and the inhabitants taken. Many were sick, the rest they took prisoner. Tamarith was able to communicate with them before the drug took effect on her, and it appears no-one is left there now."

"Then it is pointless journeying to Midgaard," Gullin said.

The slavers, if that's who they are," Vidarh went on, "apparently used a small flyer to cross the Plain of Angrboda and the mountains. They were heading south when they came across Tamarith's party at the Gunningap Pass, and veered west. They took their prisoners on board, drugged them and headed for Midgaard. That's all Tamarith was able to remember about their capture. "If I'm right about the location, their captors are probably now heading for Sleipnir. At least we know they've turned away from Gladsheim."

"We probably have Helva and Narvi to thank for that," Gullin said, "but it's terrible news about Midgaard. We can only hope we run into the raiders before they reach Sleipnir."

Vidarh's feelings bordered on relief, despite his concern for his family. At least now, one of his problems had resolved itself. Since there was no necessity to journey to Midgaard, he could make for Sleipnir without leaving the search party and feeling he was deserting his friends. Sad though he was for the inhabitants of Midgaard, it made his own situation a little easier.

"I'll contact Sleipnir before we start off again," he said. "If I can reach them I can warn them so they can defend themselves.

"Melind and I will join you," Gullin told him. "The power of three minds will reach Sleipnir more easily than one."

"The Nidhogg's Teeth Range stretches across the whole Southern Continent, doesn't it? It's not going to be easy to get through on horseback." Melind's voice betrayed her anxiety.

"I know a narrow trail over the mountains. It's a difficult crossing this far west, but these ponies are sure-footed enough. Don't worry, we'll make it." There was not a quicker way to Sleipnir and Vidarh was hopeful they would find Tamarith and her friends before the slavers reached the settlement.

Dahll and Jess had absorbed the news in silence. But now Dahll stepped forward.

"Vidarh, did Tamarith say anything about her captors...was she able to describe them to you?"

"Yes, they're definitely off-worlders. Very tall and thickset, she says, "dark eyed with shiny copper-colored skin but otherwise humanoid." He noticed Dahll and Jess exchange glances. "Tamarith thinks there are six of them altogether and their leader is female, apparently of striking appearance."

Jess frowned. "It certainly sounds like Salmaran slavers, and drugging the food to keep their prisoners unconscious would be right in character. There's one thing that puzzles me, though. From our encounters with Narjohol, we know they have a similar technology to that of the Anraatians."

Dahll nodded. "Their star drives are very similar

in design to ours, although their ships look quite different in appearance."

"Neither Earth nor Anraat, or in fact any civilised planet we've come across, has the technology to put in place a barrier such as the one that surrounds Niflheim now," Jess continued. "That means either the Salmarans have made tremendous advances in the last few years—"

"Or they're in league with a civilisation far in advance of anything we know," Dahll finished for her.

She fixed her gaze on him, her expression worried.

"Perhaps we should discuss this while we eat," Vidarh suggested. "We can't afford to lose too much of the daylight."

****

Tamarith's thoughts jumbled in confusion. Her overwhelming feeling was one of enormous relief. She had made contact and knew her family was out searching for her and the others. She could only pray the rescue party found them soon.

Strange that Vidarh should have been the one to receive her thoughts, rather than Gullin. She had never known her elder brother not to have picked up her thoughts before. Vidarh must be even more gifted than she had supposed. After her initial concern, she had to admit to herself that she was not sorry she had spoken to Vidarh. His voice in her mind had felt comforting, familiar even. She could picture his eyes, his crooked smile...

Oh, this was crazy. It was lack of nourishment and the gravity of her situation that was giving her such thoughts. She would be imagining she felt something for him next. She must clear her thoughts, try to keep her wits about her...

She heard footsteps approaching and shuddered.

Hedrohan was returning.

****

"Vidarh," Gullin said when they had finished their meal, "you know the area ahead better than any of us. How long do you estimate it will take us to reach the caves?"

"If we make good time today, I would think we'll cross Nidhogg's Teeth before sundown tomorrow."

Gullin nodded. "We will need to be careful, though. Our only chance of rescuing our people is if we can take their captors by surprise."

"Yes. With luck they'll not be expecting us to follow."

While Dahll and Jess cleared away the remnants of their meal and reloaded the packs onto the ponies, the three telepaths walked a short distance away, where they stood motionless for several minutes. Vidarh felt his mind touched by that of Gullin and Melind. Their power united with his and he sent out a message with an urgency such as he had only used once before, when he was caught in the current of the underground river on his way to Gladsheim.

People of Sleipnir, if anyone can hear me, please respond. Sleipnir is in peril. I repeat, Sleipnir is in peril.

Over and over he repeated the message, Gullin and Melind amplifying his thoughts and sending feelings of urgency and danger.

At last, he felt another mind, familiar but distant, join his own.

Vidarh. Are you about to return to us?

I'm sorry, I may not be able to return immediately, although I am on my way. How are you and Mother? Are you free of the sickness?

Yes, so far, no one has fallen sick here, but we are getting messages that it is spreading. It can only be a matter of time.

There's a chance it can be halted. We were able to

contact the off-worlders, Dahll and Jess, whose computer is developing a vaccine. But listen, Father, there is more. The captors of the party journeying back to Midgaard have overcome the settlement and we fear they are now on their way to Sleipnir. Everyone there is in danger.

Understood, my son. We have already heard that Midgaard was attacked and its people taken captive. We will not allow them to take Sleipnir, or we will die in its defence.

Vidarh passed a hand across his face. I hope it won't come to that, Father. We're aiming to catch up with the invaders and prevent them from reaching Sleipnir. If we are successful, we will rescue their captives.

You are brave, Vidarh, but do not be rash. Let Gullin guide you, he has great wisdom.

I will, Father. May the Universal Spirit protect you and our family.

As he broke contact, Vidarh turned to Gullin and Melind, shaken by the unexpected warmth in his father's words, the nearest thing to praise he'd ever received from him. For a moment, he wondered if he were doing the right thing.

Should he leave his companions and return home immediately? He would be faster alone.

His doubts faded as quickly as they had come. He would probably be of more help to his family by staying with Gullin's party and trying to prevent the slavers from reaching Sleipnir. Besides, he knew in his heart he would not be able to rest until he was sure Tamarith was safe. For to be honest, he was surprised and moved to have been the one who received her message, rather than her brother.

She had touched more than his mind, then. She had touched his heart.

****

They were able to gallop across the narrow

95

stretch of plain before the mountains and gain precious time. As the veils of mist drifted off the lower ground, they found themselves in bright sunshine.

Nidhogg's Glacier lay before them, glowing in various shades of blue against brilliant white. Skirting the huge ice mass, they hugged the base of the mountains. Here, the reed-choked grassland, littered with crumbled stone and rocky outcrops where the glacier had eaten into the ground on its endless journey, forced them to slow to a walk.

At last, they reached the narrow, twisting trail that would lead them across the mountain range. They made slow progress up the track, looking back at the blue and white of the glacier, gleaming in the sunlight and contrasting markedly with the rock's blackness, as they made the gradual climb above it. Black rock and white snow were all that lay ahead, although here and there the colour of the rocks changed to green or red as if splashed with a gigantic paintbrush.

At times, the trail petered out altogether and Vidarh, leading the way, was thankful the ponies were so sure-footed. He had spent days at a time in these mountains. Each twist and turn, each pinnacle of rock or small, misshapen tree somehow maintaining a tenuous hold on the unfriendly surface, was familiar to him.

Even so, his task was not easy. They each had a spare pony to watch, as well as their own mounts. As they rode, thoughts of Tamarith filled Vidarh's mind and he tried repeatedly to contact her, without success.

The air grew colder the higher they climbed, and he pulled his coat around him, glad of its warmth. The mist from the peaks swirled in ghostly drifts, at times so thick he could hardly see ahead of him. He had to trust his pony's instincts to avoid slipping over the edge. Sometimes the mist disappeared completely, so he could see into the valley far below. At such times, the glacier below was so dazzling it hurt his eyes to look at it.

The pinnacles of the mountains towered, black and sinister above him, so high he could not see their summits. The air, as well as growing cold, was also becoming thin. Vidarh glanced behind him to see how Dahll and Jess were coping. He was relieved to note they did not appear to be suffering from the altitude or the rarefied atmosphere.

Melind rode immediately behind him, Dahll in front of Jess, with Gullin at the end of the string and Malmooth trotting along behind. Vidarh urged his pony on a little, extending its stride. Darkness would be falling in a few hours and he wanted them to be off these mountains before then.

A plaintive, drawn-out call sounded in the still air. Vidarh stared up at the azure sky. A snow eagle soared and dipped high above him, its whiteness contrasting with the sky's deep blue, the eagle's wings tipped with black. Vidarh's attention was still on the bird when he heard a commotion behind him, a crashing and rattling of grit and boulders slamming down the mountainside.

He reined in his mount and looked back to see Melind's pack pony sliding down the face of the mountain as her mare, Melody, reared straight up on her hind legs, hoofs flailing the air. He watched in horror as the girl, losing her balance, screamed and fell from the saddle and over the edge of the precipice.

Chapter Thirteen

Vidarh!

Vidarh? she had meant to call for Gullin. Something had happened. Melind. Her sister was in trouble. She had heard a scream in her mind. Then...nothing Tamarith took a deep breath and rested her head against the hard stone wall of her prison. The last time she tried to reach her brother she had connected with Vidarh. Hardly surprising that he was in her thoughts now.

But what had happened to Melind? At that moment she would have given everything she possessed to be able to talk with Vidarh, to know they were all unharmed.

Oh Vidarh, what is happening to me? Why are you so much on my mind?

If only she were not so helpless. If only she could escape-—find the others. But there was no way to get through the forcefield, and she was growing weak. Lack of food and water was taking its toll. So far she had managed to avoid being caught getting rid of the drugged food but how long would she escape detection?

****

Vidarh and Dahll leapt off their mounts to peer down the side of the mountain. To Vidarh's relief, Melind had only fallen a few metres, and a small ledge jutting out from the main rock face had saved her from plunging to the bottom.

She lay motionless and, for a moment, Vidarh feared the worst. Then she moved her arms and shifted a little, moving perilously close to the edge of the rocky shelf, causing a flurry of stones and pebbles to clatter down the mountainside.

Melind, he telepathed, *don't move, we'll get you back up. Try to lie still.*

"Are you hurt?" Dahll called, no doubt keeping his voice low so as not to alarm her further.

"I—I think I've twisted my ankle," she shouted back and Vidarh felt the wave of fear she tried to mask through her pain.

By now, Gullin had reached them on foot. Vidarh looked back along the track and saw Jess doing her best to soothe the ponies and hold them still, at the same time trying to comfort Malmooth, who stood rigid, making little cries, almost like a dog whimpering. He turned back to Dahll, who had taken a rope from his saddle and tied it to a sharp outcrop of rock, obviously preparing to lower himself down the cliff face.

Vidarh caught hold of his arm. "No, Dahll, don't put yourself in danger. It's all right, Gullin and I will bring her up."

Gullin nodded agreement and he and Vidarh stood silently on the rim of the mountain, focusing their thoughts on the injured girl. Vidarh felt the power of Gullin's mind link with his own as they willed Melind to become weightless, visualising her drifting upward to safety. As their minds touched hers, she made a slight movement of her head, and looked down.

She jerked and gasped as she realized her danger, dislodging more stones and pebbles and almost toppling over the edge.

Vidarh concentrated all his power, still linked with Gullin's, on preventing her from falling, and then to gradually raise her to the surface. Eventually, little by little, she rose from the hard rock. Their minds connected with her own, defying gravity and causing her to float gradually up the side of the cliff face. After what seemed to Vidarh an interminable length of time, they settled her safely between them on the rough ground at the edge of the cliff.

Vidarh and Gullin locked gazes, each acknowledging their respect for the other's power, at the same time breathing a joint sigh of relief.

Gullin knelt down and raised the girl's head.

"Melind, are you all right. What happened?"

"I...I...I'm sorry. Ow!" She winced in obvious pain.

"Here, give me your arm." Dahll quickly administered what Vidarh realized was an analgesic shot. "That'll help until we're over these mountains and can treat you properly."

"How did it happen?" Gullin asked again.

"I...I'm not sure. I think a small animal shot out from under Flyer's feet, but I didn't really see it. I just felt it in my mind at the same time Flyer panicked and slipped over the edge..." She broke off with a sob, tears trailing down her face. "I'm so sorry. It's all my fault."

"No one's blaming you," Gullin said, although his expression was grim. "Accidents happen. Do you think you can ride if we help you back on Melody?"

"Yes, I'll be all right. Really."

The mare stood quietly now, and Gullin lifted Melind up and into the saddle. After helping her put her uninjured foot in the stirrup and gather up the reins, Vidarh glanced back up the trail to where Jess stood with the rest of the ponies, and waved to indicate things were under control and they were ready to move on again.

****

The grey haze of dusk descended, and with it the inevitable mist, when at last they rode down the steep mountain track and into a break in the trees that clothed the foot of the range. Vidarh followed the beam of light from Dahll's wrist flare as he swept it around and along the base of the rocky cliff behind them. "There's a series of caves here, d'you reckon it's safe to make camp in one of them tonight?"

Vidarh leapt from his pony and stood in silence for a moment. "I don't sense any danger," he said at length. "I don't think there's even an icecat lurking in *these* caves. It would probably be safer in there than making camp out in the open. At least we can light a fire without it being seen."

Gullin dismounted and lifted Melind from the saddle.

Jess came forward, eyes anxious, and looked at Melind.

"How is she? Is she badly hurt?"

"I don't think so. But if we can get her into that cave we can check her over properly."

Jess was already pulling her own sleeping roll from behind Dancer's saddle. She spread it out on the floor of the cave and Gullin carefully laid Melind onto it. The girl was now only semi-conscious and made no protest as Jess gently eased off her long, wool-lined boots.

The ankle was very swollen. "I think it's broken, not just sprained," Jess said, digging into her pack for something. Vidarh watched with interest as she ran the instrument over Melind's ankle. Jess nodded after studying the readings, before changing a setting and moving the instrument across the girl's ankle several times. A reddish light glowed, and turned blue after a few seconds.

"That should do it," Jess said. "The bone will start healing now and by tomorrow she should be able to put weight on it without pain."

Melind opened her eyes and stared around her in confusion.

"It's all right," Jess said, "you're safe. We've

101

treated your ankle and it should heal overnight."

"Th—thank you. It feels better already."

"Are you hurting anywhere else?"

"Just my hand." She held out the palm of her right hand. The delicate skin was blistered and red, where the rope had burned through her gloves as she tried to hang on to the terrified pony. Jess ran the regenerating instrument over it again and within a few minutes, only a slight scar remained.

"The scar will be gone by the morning," she promised.

Melind's eyes opened wide. "That's incredible...a miracle."

Jess chuckled. "Not quite, but it's a pretty impressive piece of equipment."

Vidarh leaned forward to inspect the instrument, and Jess demonstrated how to operate it. "Another of the Phidians' inventions," she told him. "It speeds up the body's natural healing processes. It can heal most wounds, including life-threatening ones. Its only drawback is if there's been a lot of blood lost, it takes time to recover fully."

"An amazing invention," Vidarh said. "I've never seen anything like it. Back home we only stitch wounds and use healing herbs and plant extracts to ease pain and encourage healing."

As Jess made Melind comfortable for the night, the girl's eyes filled with tears. "Flyer," she said. "It's all my fault, isn't it?"

Jess put a consoling arm around her. "These things happen. I'll give you something to help you sleep," she added. "You'll feel better when you've rested."

Melind nodded tearfully and Jess delved into her pack again. She brought out a small container of liquid, which she poured into a beaker of water and held to the girl's lips.

Seeing the girl become calmer under Jess's

capable ministration, Vidarh went with Dahll to build a fire and set up sleeping places.

After a while, Jess and Gullin joined them at the fireside. "She's sleeping now," Gullin said. He smiled at Jess. "Thank you for tending her, you are a good physician."

"It must be wonderful to have such skill," Vidarh said. "To be able to heal injuries and take away pain."

"I've had a little medical training and can cope with most common accidents or minor illnesses," Jess replied, but I don't class myself a physician. I'm very thankful to the Phidians though, they've made healing very easy."

Gullin nodded. "Their advances are well known, even as far away as Niflheim. That's why we thought of them when we were first struck by the sickness."

"I'd almost forgotten about the sickness," Jess confessed as she seated herself by the fire, next to Dahll. "We've been so intent on finding Tamarith."

"Have you or Vidarh heard anything else from her?" Dahll asked, helping himself to a steaming beaker of kobah and handing one to Jess, together with a hunk of bread and some cheese.

"No," Gullin said, "I've tried to make contact with her again but there is nothing."

Vidarh shook his head. "I've not been able to reach her either." He was more worried than he cared to admit. They were closer to the caves now and surely it should be easier to make contact.

"Vidarh," Gullin went on, "I think you and I should try to make contact with Tamarith in the morning. It will help if she can tell us how many we're going to be up against."

"I don't imagine they're expecting a rescue attempt," Vidarh commented.

"They might," Dahll said, "If they've found out

Tamarith regained consciousness long enough to transmit a message this morning."

Gullin pulled a folded map from beneath his heavy coat and consulted it for a moment, then laid it down and gestured to the others to look at it. "Vidarh, you know this area better than I do. We're here," he indicated the foothills at the base of Nidhogg's Teeth. "The western forest lies before us. How long do you calculate it will take us to pass through?"

Vidarh considered. "If we start out at first light, we should be through it by midday—"

"In that case," Dahll suggested, "it might be better to rest in the morning and start out later. That way we can go in under cover of darkness. He turned to Jess. "What about Melind, will she be fit to ride tomorrow?

Jess glanced toward the sleeping girl. "I think she should be all right. The bone should have healed by noon tomorrow. It would be better if she doesn't have to exert herself too much, though."

Dahll surveyed the group with an unusually serious expression in his eyes. "I think if the enemy we face is Salmaran, there's not much hope of that. I reckon we're in for something of a rough fight."

****

"How dare you! How dare you try to...how you say...get the better of me? Have you not learned yet that *no one*, least of all an insignificant slave, outsmarts Hedrohan!"

By the light of the globes set into the walls, the alien woman's black eyes seemed to glow in fury. She stood, legs apart, hands raised with clenched fists. She spoke *Common Universal*, the interstellar language, and although her strange accent was difficult to understand, her meaning came across plainly to the girl she towered over.

Tamarith shrank back against the wall, and

stared at Hedrohan defiantly. She braced herself for another blow. When it landed, the force of it sent her sprawling. She fell on her side, avoiding hitting her head, but the hard rock knocked the breath out of her. Her heavy clothes probably saved her from being hurt more than she was. The side of her face and her shoulders already felt swollen and bruised from the ferocity of earlier blows. She bit back a moan, determined not to let Hedrohan have the satisfaction of hearing her call out.

The woman emitted something that sounded like a wild animal's snarl, her copper-colored scaly skin shimmering in the artificial light. Before she could recover, Hedrohan twined a hank of Tamarith's long hair around her hand, and dragged her to her feet. Uttering oaths in a language Tamarith had never heard before, she jerked the young woman's head back, sending needles of pain shooting through her neck and shoulders. Tamarith gasped as the Salmaran leant close to her, her foul breath almost making her gag.

"You will pay for what you have done. Don't think you can send for help, I will make sure you never again use your powers of telepathy. You will never be found, *ever!*"

Hedrohan jerked Tamarith's head back again, and pressed a strange-smelling pad over her nose and mouth. After a momentary struggle, Tamarith descended once more into unconsciousness.

Chapter Fourteen

They spent the morning discussing tactics and making the most of the time to rest. Several times Vidarh went out into the mist-shrouded clearing with Gullin. Together they focussed their minds in an attempt to make contact with Tamarith, but each time there was no response.

Vidarh remembered the first time Tamarith and he had linked minds. She had been assigned to guide him safely to Gladsheim. The distance here to the mountain caves was no more than it had been when he was on the plain of Angrboda, yet he could sense nothing from her. Yesterday, he had been the one she contacted. Why could he not reach her now, when they were closer?

Once they were back inside the cave, he saw Jess and Dahll squatting down, studying the map with Melind, who had slept for most of the morning, peering over their shoulders.

"Are you feeling better, Melind?" Gullin asked.

"Yes, thank you. My ankle's hardly hurting at all and my hand's completely healed. Look!" She held up her hand, which was unblemished with no sign of a rope burn.

"We've been talking about Loki's Chasm," Jess said. "It sounds like a place to avoid, if what Melind says is true."

"Not that I've ever seen it," the girl put in hastily, "but all the stories I've heard make it sound pretty frightening."

"It is," Vidarh agreed. "The legends say it's bottomless and anyone who falls into it is lost forever. We shouldn't need to go near it. It's beneath the mountains of the Hela Range, west of Sleipnir. It's not that far from the settlement. The caves where Tamarith said she and the others are being held lie to the west, through the forest, about twenty-three kilometres away from the chasm itself." He looked around. "If everyone's agreeable, I suggest we get going. Once we're through the forest we can wait until it's dark to make our move."

"I'm ready." Dahll stood, and caught hold of Jess's hands, pulling her to her feet.

"I'll fetch the ponies," Vidarh said. It did not take him long to round up the animals foraging at the edge of the trees. He found the icecat nearby nibbling at any tender shoots brave enough to emerge from the cold, snow-covered earth. By the time he returned leading the string of ponies, the others were waiting with their packs prepared and their saddles and bridles laid out ready. In a short space of time they were all mounted, and prepared to make their way through the forest.

The darkness under the trees lay heavy and eerily quiet. The mist, filtering down through the branches stung cold and wet against Vidarh's skin. No birdsong disturbed the silence and no animals moved in the undergrowth. Patchy layers of snow, thinly covering the layer of dead needles from the trees, carpeted the ground, and their ponies' hooves made no sound as they moved through the forest. The air smelt damp, full of the scent of earth and decayed leaves.

Vidarh shivered, although his thick coat and the furry hat pulled down over his ears prevented even the chilliest winds from penetrating. There was a sense of desolation under these trees, which was quite different from the atmosphere in the woods clothing the mountains further south.

From time to time he glanced back, measuring

his pony's stride to match those of the others, making sure they were all within his range of vision. He did not intend to risk another accident if he could avoid it. Melind seemed to have recovered from her ordeal, but he kept a watchful eye on her, frequently turning in his saddle to check all was well.

When at last the trees began to thin out, Vidarh reined in his pony and signalled to the others to do the same. "We're not far from the caves now. We'd best halt here until dusk," he said. "We don't want to be spotted before we've even had a chance to spy out the area."

"We'll unsaddle the ponies and hide our packs," Gullin said. "Best turn the ponies loose, and send them back through the forest."

They piled their supplies and saddles under the trees while Dahll used his laser cutter to chop off the lower branches of some of the smaller trees to cover them.

"How long will we have to wait?" Jess asked as they settled themselves down on the ground.

"It's not long until dusk," Vidarh said. "It might be wise for the rest of you to stay here, while I work my way to where I can see the caves and check out what's going on. I'm used to stalking. I can creep up on them without them hearing me."

"I'll come with you," Gullin and Dahll said together.

"I want to come too," Melind said. "I'm fine now and I'm tired of sitting around waiting."

Vidarh shook his head. "It would be best if no more than two go, we'll be less likely to be seen."

"Then we'll stay here while you and Gullin reconnoitre," Dahll said. "You should have someone here to cover your back, just in case."

"What about me?" Melind protested, "I don't want to stay behind again."

"Better that you stay with Jess and Dahll until

we call you to join us," Gullin said firmly.

The girl looked less than happy, but Vidarh was glad her brother had made her stay with Dahll and Jess. She would probably have to fight soon enough and despite her claims about her recovery, it would be better for her to conserve her strength until needed.

****

They travelled the short distance to the caves while there was still a little light, although wisps of mist were already beginning to curl down from the mountains like wraiths of silver smoke.

Flattening themselves on their bellies, Gullin and Vidarh inched their way forward to the edge of the forest. Vidarh raised his head cautiously, and surveyed the area in front of the cliffs. Three tall other-worlders stood in front of a large overland vehicle. Two men and a woman. The woman seemed to be the one giving orders, although he did not understand the words she used. They loaded a group of confused-looking prisoners into the vehicle. Tied together, with their hands bound, they moved slowly, barely lifting their feet, and seemed scarcely aware of what was happening to them.

It looks like they are being taken back to the ferry vehicle. Gullin telepathed beside him.

They'll probably hold them there until they've captured as many as they can, then fly them all back to the main ship when it returns.

Returns?

It's not orbiting the planet at the moment, or Jess and Dahll's ship would have detected it.

Perhaps it is the main ship that controls the space barrier preventing our friends from leaving. We need to summon the others, Gullin replied, as the vehicle disappeared from their view.

They united their minds and transmitted a message to Melind.

****

"What's the position?" Dahll whispered a short while later, as he squatted next to Vidarh and peered through the reedy grass to squint into the shadows.

"From what Tamarith told us before," Vidarh whispered back, "it would seem the captives are all held in the caves here. The leader of the gang and two of her men have taken off in some kind of transport vehicle with some prisoners, and we assume they're heading for their ferry ship, wherever that is."

"There's one guard outside the entrance to the caves," Gullin added. "We're not sure how many others are inside with the prisoners."

"We'd best wait until the moon's up before we move in," Dahll said, "Our wrist flares will attract too much attention and we need to have some light."

"Have you managed to contact Tamarith yet?" Melind asked, her voice betraying her anxiety.

"Not yet," Gullin answered. "We tried a few times while we were waiting for you to join us but so far, nothing."

Vidarh could feel the tension emanating from both the girl and her brother. "Why don't we try again," he suggested. "There must be a reason we've not been able to reach her...we have to keep on trying until we do."

Gullin turned to Dahll and Jess who crouched behind him in the darkness. "You will excuse us please, while we try? We need to contact her."

"Of course," Jess whispered back. "I just wish Dahll and I could help."

"You already are, just by being with us."

****

Where was she? Tamarith opened her eyes and eased herself to a standing position. There nothing. The blackness was complete, not a glimmer of light anywhere. She blinked and gulped down the panic that once more swept over her. She should be used to waking up alone in the dark by now. She would not allow herself to succumb to her fear. The darkness itself could not hurt her. It was Hedrohan who was her enemy.

How long had it been since their captors had lain in ambush for them, killing Lars and capturing everyone else? Keeping track of time was difficult when she had not seen daylight for so long. The only indication she had was the meal which the guards brought daily.

She reached out her hands and they met jagged, damp stone walls. She groped around with her fingers, stretching them out until she found a part of the rock that was smoother than the rest. With measured, slow movements, she felt along the wall and moved along it gradually. She sensed the energy barrier before her and moved back a little, working her way sideways to the opposite wall, gauging her steps. It did not take long for her to reach the smooth area of rock once more. At least now, she had an idea of the size and limitations of her prison. There was no way out. The invisible wall of energy before her in the darkness was impenetrable.

The side of her face was tender and it took a moment for her to remember why. She had a metallic taste in her mouth, and the heat and soreness in her lips when she touched them told her they must be swollen and bruised. She licked them cautiously, and realized the taste was her own blood.

Hedrohan seemed to enjoy making her suffer and found new ways of hurting her each time she visited her prisoners. Apart from that one time, however, she had made sure she left no marks where they would be clearly visible.

Slowly Tamarith slid to a crouching position and buried her head in her hands. Had Hedrohan guessed her fear of the dark and left her here as punishment? Or perhaps she'd been left in the dark to make sure she had no idea where she was. To ensure that even if she made contact, she could not tell the others where to find her.

Before Hedrohan had administered another drug to render Tamarith once more unconscious, she had overheard snippets of conversation between Hedrohan and the guards. It seemed they had taken some of the other prisoners to their transport vehicle. They must be on their way back by now. Would she be moved to the transporter, too? If only she had some means of gauging the time, so at least she could prepare herself for the slaver's return.

A suspicion crept into her mind. What if her captors had abandoned her? What if she were never found? She would die here alone, never seeing her home or family again.

Tamarith forced herself to breathe deeply. Such thoughts were foolish. She was in a deeper part of the cave network, that was all. Hedrohan might rough her up a bit, but she would hardly leave a slave to die. Slaves brought money.

She peered through the darkness, trying to discern some shadow in the gloom, some indication that she was not alone, but there was nothing.

She recalled her conversation with Vidarh the morning after he had arrived at Gladsheim, when she had told him about her fear of the dark. She remembered him telling her everyone was afraid of something. Somehow it was a comfort.

Thinking of her home and her conversation with Vidarh was far better than allowing her imagination to conjure up horrors in the dark to cloud her mind, but the question still remained—why had Vidarh been the first to receive her message on the morning of her abduction? Of course he had exceptional powers. He could teleport further than anyone she had ever heard of, and she suspected his telepathic abilities were greater than average as well.

She dismissed the wayward idea that sneaked into her mind, whispering that perhaps there was also a physical attraction, which could be strengthening their mutual telepathic abilities. Then again, he was certainly more attractive to think about than Hedrohan.

Once more she visualised his face with its strong contours and kind, hazel eyes. She almost imagined she could hear his voice telling her to be strong, not to give up.

She breathed in deeply, and, casting her mind beyond the walls of her rocky prison, visualised the snowy landscape, and reached out to her brother and the others searching for her. She needed to contact them before Hedrohan came back and forced her to board the transporter or she might be lost forever.

****

Keeping out of sight of the Salmarans, Vidarh, Melind and Gullin knelt together, rigid in concentration. Vidarh closed his eyes and they sent out a joint message: *Tamarith we are outside the caves. Can you hear us? Please...answer us if you can. Tamarith, please answer.*

Three times they repeated the message, then emptied their minds of all thoughts, to be receptive to any response. Several minutes passed with no result. Vidarh glanced at Gullin, who gave an almost imperceptible nod. Again they broadcast their message, again they waited. A warmth began to fill his mind, a presence. At last, he could feel her mind in his.

Tamarith!

Vidarh, Gullin—and Melind—I was afraid something had happened. Can you hear me? Am I reaching you?

Yes, we can hear you. Are you all right? Vidarh

wondered if she could feel his relief, in the same way he felt that of Gullin and Melind as they united their thoughts with his.

Yes...although Hedrohan, the leader, was not pleased when she found I'd avoided eating the drugged food she gave us.

Vidarh shuddered at the visions that came to him, of the savage other-worlder beating Tamarith without mercy. Tamarith must have known some of her pain would come across, despite her obvious attempt to hide it. He forced his mind not to dwell on it. It would not help her if he projected back his own feelings of anxiety and anger over what she must have endured.

Are you here, in the caves?

We've been moved from the caves we were in first. They blindfolded us, but we did not move very far and I sense we are still in the Nidhogg's Teeth range. Hedrohan's isolated me from the others. She drugged me again. When she realized we weren't eating the doped food they brought us, she started injecting us instead. She's been gone a while though, and it must have worn off.

How many Salmarans are there guarding you? Vidarh asked.

Two. They come and check on me at intervals, then go back to guard the rest of the prisoners. From what I could gather from their conversations, I believe there is another guarding the entrance. The Salmaran leader and the other two apparently left with some prisoners a while ago.

We saw them. Don't worry Tamarith, we'll get you out of there. Vidarh felt Gullin's mind combine with his own, and realized most of the conversation with Tamarith had been conducted through himself. Before he could contemplate on this, she came back to him.

Thank you. I knew you and the others would not

give up on us. A pause: *Vidarh—*
Yes, Tamarith?
Please...hurry.

The plea wrenched at Vidarh's heart. He could tell she was trying to sound strong and confident, but her torment, the fear she tried desperately to suppress, sent echoes of despair through every nerve in his body.

He risked a brief, mental hug of reassurance. *We're coming, Tamarith, stay strong. Try to keep in contact with us. We'll be there as soon as we can.*

As Tamarith's voice drifted out of his mind, Vidarh turned to his companions. *Well at least we know she's alive and conscious.* He stopped as he noticed the puzzled expressions on their faces.

You were able to talk to her!

Yes, weren't you? I felt all four of our minds uniting—

Gullin glanced at Melind as if for confirmation that her experience was the same as his. *We heard her, but not as clearly as you obviously did, she seemed far away...distant. I fear she must be very weak.*

She's all right though, isn't she? Melind looked at Vidarh, her dark eyes full of anxiety. *I mean I heard her but I couldn't get through to her, myself.*

You're weak too, Melind, and not at your best for difficult transmissions. Tamarith seems to be very deep within the mountain caves and she's been drugged, to dull her mind. It's amazing she was able to reach us at all. I've told her we're on our way to rescue her.

****

"Jess—did you get something from Tamarith?"

"Yes, Dahll. Yes, I did. She came through very faintly, I've heard her much more clearly at other times, but at least she's alive, and that's the main thing."

"You spoke to her?"

"No, but I felt her in my mind."

"You heard her, too?"

Jess turned at Vidarh's voice. "I got something from her, certainly. Did she speak to you?"

"Yes, and Gullin and Melind heard her as well."

"She is weak," Gullin replied, "her thoughts reached me but faintly, although I believe she came through to Vidarh more strongly than to either Melind or myself."

Briefly, he recapped Tamarith's ordeal for Jess and Dahll. "When she worked out what was happening she avoided eating the food brought to her. We were right, there are two guards and they're using several of the caves deep in the mountain to hold their captives. It seems she has been moved to another cave deeper still, as punishment for evading the drugged food."

"All we have to do is get rid of the guard outside the entrance and overpower the two guarding the prisoners. Then we can rescue them," Dahll stated with a hint of irony in his voice. "The odds are pretty much in our favour, at least."

"At the moment," Gullin agreed, "but we need to move quickly before the others get back."

"How are we going to sneak up on the guard and overcome him without him seeing us?" Melind asked.

Jess glanced through the trees at the moon, fully risen and casting a pearly pink light across the clearing now that the mist had dissipated.

"I'll show you." She rose cautiously to her feet and slipped down the hood of the white Phidian cloak, which she wore over her thermal suit. Shaking her long hair so it cascaded seductively about her shoulders she stepped forward.

Vidarh reached out to stop her.

"It's all right," Dahll said quietly. "It's not the first time Jess and I have been in this kind of situation. She knows what she's doing." He waved his blaster. "I have her covered if anything goes wrong."

Jess strode across the clearing. When she was half way, she stopped, as if startled.

"Oh."

The guard had seen her and now stood to attention, his hand on his weapon.

"Thank the Universal Spirit you're here," she called, "I'm lost." Her breathless tones in the still air sounded vulnerable and she looked around, giving the impression of being nervous and scared.

He shuffled toward her until he was a metre or so away, and shouted something in a language Vidarh had never heard before.

"Will you help me?" she asked, and tilted her head so her hair swirled around her, catching the moonlight and shimmering like molten copper. At the same time, she casually let her long cape slip back over her shoulders, as if to show she was not wearing a weapon. The tight-fitting thermal suit beneath, revealed her feminine curves to their full advantage. "I'll make it worth your while."

Vidarh could not help smiling. She was good...and she did indeed seem to know what she was doing.

The Salmaran stopped and let his gaze roam over her figure.

"Do you speak common universal?" she asked.

"What you do out here?" he asked in a gruff voice, stepping closer.

Vidarh had wondered what would happen if Jess could not make herself understood.

"I'm looking for some friends," she replied, letting her cloak fall to the ground.

As the Salmaran stepped forward, reaching out his arm, Jess grabbed it and stepped forward, hooking her leg behind his. Bending her knee and twisting her body, she threw him over her back and onto his, while wrenching his gun from his hand. An instant later she straddled his body, then fired a thin stunner beam at the slaver's head.

"There," she said, and picked up her cloak as Vidarh and the others hurried to her side. "That should keep him quiet for a while. It may be the oldest trick in the Cosmos, but it hasn't failed me yet."

Vidarh gave her an admiring smile, and Dahll hugged her briefly, with a nod toward the cave entrance.

"I reckon we'd better get this rescue operation started."

Chapter Fifteen

"We can't just dive into the caves blind," Jess said. "We know there are at least two Salmarans on guard, but we have no idea where the prisoners are located."

"There is a line of communication between us and Tamarith now," Vidarh said. "We will know when we are getting close."

"We need to have someone on guard here," Dahll stated. "Jess and I have had more experience at this sort of thing. It makes sense for us to go in there and for two of you to stay outside on guard. If the Salmarans come back, at least you'll be able to warn us, without the risk of attracting their attention by using a communicator."

Gullin nodded reluctantly. "Melind and I will stay on guard here, with Malmooth. Vidarh, will you go with Jess and Dahll?"

"Of course. I can keep in touch with the two of you telepathically and—"

"But I want to go too," Melind pouted. "It's not fair. I always have to stay behind. I don't want to wait here and miss all the action."

A look from Gullin silenced her. "You're more use here. And you don't want to risk getting injured again."

Melind scowled, but refrained from arguing further with her brother.

"We'll contact you every three minutes," Vidarh said. "Unless we need to make contact immediately."

"Likewise," Gullin said.

With a brief nod, Dahll led the group into the

caverns. They moved forward cautiously. As they descended deeper into the caves, Vidarh noticed Jess shiver and snuggle into her cloak, pulling the hood back up over her head. He drew his own outer garment more closely around him. The raw cold settled over them like a cloud. Large, hexagonal lighting units placed strategically in the rock at intervals provided just enough illumination for them to see their way. The huge, distorted shadows they cast leapt from the walls, and caused the trio to jump back every now and then, blasters at the ready. Helicites reached out in all directions, like strangely misshapen claws, and massive, discolored stalagmites rose up from the cave floor, dwarfing them.

The caves grew narrower, and damp underfoot, as they progressed. The biting cold increased. Gigantic stalagmites reached upward like icy pillars, and thin, twisted, stalactites hung down from the roof of the caverns, but had none of the magical quality of those in the caves in the mountains bordering the Drasil Plain.

After walking for what seemed like much longer than the few minutes Jess assured him it actually was, Vidarh stopped abruptly. With a tingle of excitement tinged with relief, he answered the voice in his mind: *Tamarith, we're in the caves, we can't be too far from you now.*

"What's up?" Jess asked, almost colliding with him.

"I'm getting something from Tamarith," Vidarh said, his voice barely rising above a whisper. "We must be getting close."

"I heard something too...or thought I did, but I couldn't make much sense of it," Jess said, keeping her voice low. "Were you able to get back to her?"

"Yes, I let her know we're on our way."

"We'd better be even more cautious from here

on," Dahll said, "if we really are getting close to Tamarith, we might run into the Salmarans as well."

"I'll just contact Gullin and Melind, to make sure they're safe."

Vidarh stood still for a moment or two, and concentrated. When he received a response from Gullin that all was quiet outside the caves, they continued along the passage in single file, keeping close to the walls, blasters drawn.

They were deep inside the labyrinth of caves now. Gradually Vidarh began to feel they were very near to Tamarith. He heard her in his mind, faintly at first, then more clearly.

Vidarh, all of you, be careful. I feel your closeness, but there are guards. Please don't come any nearer, you are in danger.

"Did you just get another message from Tamarith?" Jess whispered.

"Yes, I did. I think we're close."

As they walked on, they heard the sound of falling water, and rounding a bend, saw a torrent pouring down from the roof ahead of them, the spray dancing in arcs of brightness in the light from the units set into the rocky cliffs on each side. The water fell into a deep chasm and when Vidarh shone his wrist-flare into it, they could see it raging far below.

"Now what do we do?" Jess asked.

"There's a narrow ledge that skirts the fall," Dahll pointed out, shining his own flare to the right of the cataract. "The Salmarans must have gone that way, with their prisoners. There doesn't seem to be any other way forward."

They made their way in single file along the ledge, taking care to keep their balance on the slippery surface. At one point, the ledge petered out altogether and they had to jump across the intervening space. It was not wide, but perilous in the half-light. The spray soaked their faces and clothing and was so cold it stung like hail. At last, they reached the other side and Jess shook the water from her long cloak. Vidarh was grateful his icecat coat had kept out the worst of the spray.

They walked in silence, stopping every now and then for Vidarh to concentrate on relaying messages to Gullin and Tamarith. After one such pause, they rounded a corner and found themselves looking across a large cavern, with smaller alcoves at the back and the black expanse of a small lake. There were more light-units here, and two Salmaran guards stood with their backs toward them.

They flattened themselves against the wall.

"Ready?" Vidarh whispered, turning to Jess and Dahll. They nodded and the three stepped into the open, blasters aimed at the Salmarans.

"Drop your weapons," Dahll commanded.

The Salmarans jerked around, but before they could fire, received the full blast of the stunner beams. Scrambling over the inert bodies, the three rescuers made for the caves at the back of the main cavern.

"How long will they be out?" Vidarh asked, glancing back at the prone figures.

"Long enough for us to rescue Tamarith and the others, I hope," Dahll said, then stopped.

Vidarh followed the direction of his gaze. Three smaller alcoves were visible, in the main chamber. Several still figures lay in each, none of whom, to his concern, was Tamarith. There were no restraints of any kind and the entrances appeared to be open. As Vidarh was about to comment on the fact, he again felt Tamarith in his mind, and looking toward Jess and Dahll, was aware they had also experienced the contact.

You must leave. You can't help us now. They...they will be returning. You must leave before they catch you, too.

What's stopping you from escaping? Vidarh asked, *and how far are you from the others?* He drew near to the cave entrance and cautiously stretched out a hand. Immediately, he leapt back, shaking his hand and putting it to his lips.

Dahll stretched out his own hand, even more cautiously, with the same result. "Forcefield," he said as Jess edged beside him.

"That explains a lot. I was wondering why they were just sitting there."

I have contact with the rest of the prisoners now. The drug's wearing off most of us here, so we are probably the next group they intend to transport to their ferry. Of course they can't move us if we're unconscious. I'm not sure where I am...when Hedrohan discovered I had informed my fellow prisoners about the food being drugged she threw me into this cave, away from the others. I can't break through the forcefield.

Don't worry, we'll get you out of there. Vidarh looked at Dahll. "Is there any way you can disable the forcefield?"

Dahll was already looking up at the rocky cliff that formed the chambers. "I'd have to find the power source. It can't be that easy to hide." A moment later, he strode over to a large boulder. "Ah-hah!" He glanced back. "Vidarh, can you give me a hand with this?"

Between them, they managed to move the stone a short distance away from the cliff face.

Jess turned toward the passage from which they had just come, to keep watch.

Dahll gave a low cry of triumph. Hidden in a niche behind the rock was a contraption that appeared to be the forcefield generator.

"Do you think you can deactivate it?" Vidarh asked.

Dahll studied the contrivance closely. "If I can

figure out whether it's booby trapped."

Jess looked over her shoulder. "Do you think it might be?"

"That's what I'd do. Although..." Dahll squinted as he inspected the device cautiously, "I would hope anything I came up with would not be so clumsy." He reached under his coat and produced a small sonic cutter. "'Course the trick is to disable it *without* setting anything off."

"Perhaps I can help," Vidarh suggested. "Don't forget we're telekinetic as well as telepathic—Wait." Vidarh was startled to receive an urgent message transmitted from Gullin.

Get out quickly. The Salmarans have returned with their transporter.

How many of them are there...are they the same ones we saw before? Are you close enough to see? Vidarh asked.

Yes, there is the woman...and the two men.

You and Melind take cover. Don't worry about us. We'll handle things here.

The captives were starting to stir and sit up now. Tamarith had been right about the effects of the drug wearing off. Vidarh looked at Jess and Dahll, who confirmed they, too, had received Gullin's message.

"We'd best take cover," Jess said, dodging behind one of the tall pillar formations. "Dahll, please, there's no time to try deactivating that now."

With a frustrated glance toward the generator, Dahll followed suit, gesturing to Vidarh to do the same.

A sharp cry echoed in Vidarh's mind, and when he tried to reach Gullin again, he felt nothing, and received no reply, nor could he contact Melind.

After several minutes of trying to contact them, he was reaching out to Tamarith again, when the three Salmarans stepped into the light and onto the rimstone bordering the pool.

One of the men had the motionless body of Gullin over his shoulder and the other carried Melind in the same manner, his bulk and tremendous height making the young woman look like a small child. A dart protruded from the girl's shoulder and Vidarh groaned inwardly as he realized she and Gullin were probably under the influence of the same drug that had subdued Tamarith and the others.

The Salmarans stopped when they saw the prone bodies of the two guards, and deposited Gullin and Melind on the ground. Stooping, the woman took what looked like a hypo-syringe from under her coat of coarse animal hair, pressed it to the arm of each of the unconscious guards, then struck out with a large leather boot, kicking them hard. As they scrambled unsteadily to their feet, she spoke in a harsh, guttural voice. Vidarh recognised the language as the same one used by the man Jess had overcome earlier.

At that moment, Dahll aimed his blaster at the nearest guard, who went down with a strangled yell. The other Salmarans leapt for cover, and for several minutes, the caves echoed with the sound of blaster fire.

Green and purple light shimmered and bounced off the surface of the pool in vivid bursts of colour, and wraiths of smoke filled the air with choking fumes.

They kept up the barrage for what seemed to be hours, but was in fact only a few minutes. There was a scream as another of the slavers fell and Vidarh began to feel that, despite their disadvantage in numbers, they might have a chance of gaining the upper hand.

The thought had no sooner come to him than he saw Dahll fling himself to one side, before collapsing upon the stone floor.

"Dahll!"

Jess threw herself down beside him and Vidarh plunged forward...

To find himself staring into the dangerous end of a blaster wielded by the Salmaran woman herself.

Chapter Sixteen

Vidarh froze, his attention riveted on the Salmaran woman. With copper-colored skin and black eyes, she was handsome by most standards. Thick black hair hung halfway down her back. As tall as her male companions, with broad shoulders and a muscular physique, her leather-clad figure gave the impression of being lithe, and at the same time, very powerful. Vidarh was only vaguely aware of the other two Salmarans beside him, hauling Jess to her feet. He had a momentary urge to fire his blaster at Hedrohan, point blank, but realized her two accomplices would probably shoot Jess as well as himself, in retaliation.

"Put down your weapon. At once!" the woman commanded in Common Universal, spoken with a strong accent.

Vidarh complied with ill grace.

The Salmaran woman nodded in the direction of the furthest alcove. One of her men moved toward it and aimed a small device at the boulder where Dahll had tried to disable the forcefield generator. At a word from Hedrohan, the other Salmaran removed Jess's weapon from her belt, and threw it into the depths of the pool.

When Dahll attempted to rise, she divested him of his weapon as well, and it followed Jess's into the black water.

"I am Hedrohan, daughter of Zolmovan, kinswoman of Narjohol. You are now my slaves. You will obey me without question." Vidarh noticed a look pass between Jess and Dahll. The next moment

Dahll's expression turned to a grimace, as Hedrohan grasped him roughly by the shoulder and called to one of her men.

"Throw them into the end cells. I'll attend to them later. It will give me much pleasure to give this one what he deserves," she added, as a Salmaran hauled Dahll to his feet.

Vidarh felt something hard prod him in the back. They were herded toward several empty recesses in front of the pool. Then a heavy booted foot slammed him into the nearest hollow. Losing his footing on the uneven ground, he fell forward on the hard ground. The two male Salmarans dragged the unconscious bodies of Gullin and Melind and set them down in the niche next to him. A low hum sounded as they activated the forcefield, then silence.

It took him a few moments to regain his senses and realize the Salmaran leader had left them. He staggered to his feet, and tried to contact Gullin and Melind.

Where are you, Jess? he telepathed, sensing her close proximity, although his vision was obscured by walls of stone on each side. "I can't seem to rouse Gullin, or his sister."

"I think they'll be out for a while yet."

Vidarh used all his concentration to hear her. It was her thoughts that came across to him, rather than her voice. Without violating the code of non-intrusion, he reached out to the periphery of her mind, just enough to amplify her words in his mind.

"Dahll's barely conscious. It looks like their blasters weren't set to full force, thank the Universal Spirit, but his wound's pretty nasty all the same."

Vidarh strained his senses as he heard her scrabbling around as if looking for something.

"Oh no! The bio-regenerator's not working, it must have got wet when we went past the waterfall.

It looks like there's a small hole in my pack where the water got in." Silence for a moment, then "Dahll. Dahll—where's you regenerator? Dahll, answer me—please."

Another silence. In his mind he heard Dahll whisper faintly "Pocket of...my coat." The pain came across as well and Vidarh winced involuntarily.

After a moment there was a muffled exclamation of despair.

"That one's wet too," Jess said in exasperation. "D'you think it'll work after it's dried out?"

"Not sure...very delicate."

Jess again. "You're losing blood and it'll take a long time for that arm to heal without a regenerator. I've nothing to bandage you with, either. Everything's wet." For the first time since he'd met her, Vidarh sensed fear, although not for herself.

"We've got to find a way out of here, Vidarh, we have to."

Vidarh's mind raced. He had an idea. There was a possibility...but would he be able to do it?

He couldn't even suggest it at the moment though. First he had to check on Tamarith.

Tamarith, am I still reaching you?

Yes, Vidarh. I hear you.

There's been some trouble here. Hedrohan returned sooner than we expected. We've been captured, but I have a plan. Will you be all right until we can figure out a way to rescue you?

Of course. All at once, he had a vision of her smile and those devastating dark eyes. *I'm not thinking of going anywhere.* The irony came across, with a sense of forlornness as well, and he sent as much reassurance as he could. She was putting on a brave front but her attempt at shielding her despondency from him had not been very successful.

He turned his thoughts back to Jess. *Have you any more regenerators?*

"Yes, but they're on board the hopper. Even if we could escape, it would take so long to reach it without the ponies and we can't round them up in the dark—"

I have an idea. Do you trust me?

"Of course I do, but—"

Enough to let me enter your mind?

She hesitated for just a moment. "I've done it before...a long time ago, with Tamarith and Gullin, but what exactly are you planning?"

I'm not sure if it will work, and that's why you need to trust me. It could be dangerous, but—he paused, wondering how to put his idea into words. Jess had proved herself courageous and resourceful but she wasn't a telepath. Even though he sensed she was far more receptive than most non-telepaths, he was still not sure what her reaction would be.

He looked across the cell. The shimmering distortion caused by the forcefield, invisible from the other side, was not too great to prevent him from seeing out. Neither of the two men Hedrohan had left on guard was close enough to overhear, if sound could even travel through the field. They appeared deep in conversation, but Vidarh couldn't hear them. Maybe they couldn't hear the prisoners, either.

I've been developing the art of...teleportation. I don't know if it will work, but if we link minds, I might be able to transport us both to the hopper.

"We have to do something. I don't want to leave Dahll, but—"

I understand, Vidarh hoped his voice in her mind was reassuring, *but we shouldn't be long and I need you to come with me. You know where the regenerators are on the hopper, and I assume you can deactivate your ship's safety device?*

"Yes. But what about the guards?"

They won't be expecting us to escape through the forcefield. Now—stand away from the wall—- and it

*would help if you could visualise your surroundings
and keep the picture in your mind.*

Concentrating all his thoughts on visualising
the recess where Jess was, and drawing what he
could from her mind, Vidarh closed his eyes-—and
took a leap into darkness.

Despite his warning, Jess started when he
appeared in front of her but was quick to regain her
composure. "I've never actually seen anyone do that,
although I knew it was possible."

She bent over Dahll. "Hang on there Dahll.
Vidarh and I are going back to the hopper. We need
to get a regenerator that works."

She gave him a soft kiss, then straightened up
and turned to Vidarh.

"All right, I'm ready."

"I'll take good care of her," Vidarh promised,
hoping Dahll could hear him. "We'll be back before
you know it." He took both Jess's hands, looking
deep into her eyes.

"Jess, think about the hopper, where you left it.
Focus your thoughts on it and think of nothing else.
Clear your mind of everything except that. Let your
mind join with mine."

For a minute or two, he braced himself as the
jumble of her emotions hit his unprotected mind.
Fear, for her lifemate, and also for Tamarith and her
siblings. Loathing for the alien woman who had
captured them and injured Dahll...and love; the love
for Dahll that overwhelmed all other emotions.

He felt the tumult in her mind while she tried to
focus as he instructed her. At last, her eyes, still
locked on his, grew clear as pools of dark green
liquid crystal, as still and as calm. He saw in her
mind the coppice where they had left the hopper,
and concentrated until he could see every detail of
the vehicle. He looked beyond it, to the trees and the
undergrowth, until he and Jess shared the same

picture in their minds.

Are you ready? he asked.

"Yes," she said, so quietly he could barely hear her, although she need not have spoken aloud.

Then hold on to my hands, concentrate on the image in your mind that we both see...and let's go.

Again the black vortex, a whirling, bitter cold, and then they stood in the darkness before a shadow looming under the trees.

Vidarh realized he was still holding Jess's hands. He let go, and turned on his wrist flare, bringing it to full beam very slowly, just in case they were not alone. The shadow revealed itself as the hopper. He looked at Jess, also adjusting her flare.

"Are you all right, you're not feeling any ill effects?"

"That was amazing!" She turned toward the hopper and busied herself with the anti-intrusion device. After a few minutes, she stepped back.

"There, that's got it." She climbed inside and activated the control panel in the front. Immediately it lit up, illuminating the inside of the vehicle. "Good, it's fully charged again." She touched another panel and the flap dropped down to expose a small cavity containing three bio-regenerators.

"Thank goodness we brought some spares from the *Quest,*" she said, putting two of the regenerators into her pack and handing one to Vidarh. She opened another compartment and withdrew several blasters. "These will replace the ones Hedrohan took." She glanced at Vidarh. "You'll be able to get us back into the cave again?"

"Of course. It should be easier this time, since you've done it before."

"With a bit of luck Hedrohan won't even know we've been gone." She secured the vehicle and set up the security system again, before standing in front of Vidarh. He took her hands in his once more and held her gaze.

"This time, think of the cave where Hedrohan held us."

He visualised the dark hollow at the back of the cavern, and waited until Jess's vision matched his. He concentrated his mind and willed them both back. Again the cold darkness...the whirling vortex, then he felt the hard stone beneath his feet and they stood outside the cells that had confined them. He released Jess's hands and looked across at her, in the light of his wrist flare.

Neither of them spoke. Vidarh stared around in disbelief.

There were no lights.

The cavern was empty.

The prisoners were gone.

Chapter Seventeen

Jess looked at Vidarh in fear and consternation. All she could think of was Dahll. He needed her. Without treatment, he could die. She fought down the rising panic that threatened to engulf her. She would not let herself think that way. He was her lifemate, her husband, and she knew him better than she knew anyone. They had a link between them that was almost as powerful as telepathy. He was strong, he'd faced death before. He was a survivor. But where was he? Where were the other prisoners?

She realized Vidarh looked as worried as she felt. She suspected his concern went even deeper than anxiety for his friends.

"It looks like Hedrohan came back and found us missing and decided to move in case we returned with reinforcements. Can you try contacting them...Tamarith?"

"I've already tried. I can't reach her. They must have taken her with the other prisoners, unless she's been drugged again."

His eyes held a dark expression of frustration. "If only I'd tried to find her first...we could have rescued her, taken her with us."

"You were concerned about Dahll," Jess said, trying to reassure him, although her own mind was in turmoil. "You weren't to know Hedrohan would come back so soon and remove the captives. Can you get through to any of the others?"

Vidarh shook his head. "I'm not getting anything from anyone. Still, I think we should try to find the cave where Tamarith was held," Vidarh said. "In case she's still there but can't communicate for some reason."

"Yes, of course." Despite her resolve, Jess realized to her dismay there were tears in her eyes. She blinked them back and turned away quickly, but not quickly enough.

Vidarh placed a reassuring hand on her arm. "Jess, we'll find them. I know how worried you are about Dahll, but I'm sure he'll be all right."

"Will he? Vidarh, he's hurt and losing blood—"

She stopped, unable to go on. A surge of warmth swept over her and she knew Vidarh had sent a wave of comfort and understanding into her mind. After a moment, she turned back to him. "I...I don't know what I'd do if I lost him...I couldn't go on without him. He's part of me."

"I know," Vidarh said. "I couldn't help realising how deep your love for each other is, when we merged minds."

She straightened and offered him a knowing look in return. "And it's not just me who's worrying about losing someone."

By the light of her wrist flare, she saw the startled expression on Vidarh's face and knew her guess was right.

She spotted her cloak still on floor of the nearest alcove, which had recently held them. She picked it up and shook it out. It was almost dry, although the air in the cavern was cold. She wondered fleetingly what material the cloak was made from. She had worn it frequently since leaving Phidia, and no matter how dirty or wet it got, it always seemed to restore itself after a short while.

"It works both ways, you know," she said, as they hurried down the narrow passage leading past the alcoves. "When we joined minds, I saw your secret thoughts too, just for a moment, but enough for me to realize there's someone you care about more than you let on."

A wry smile crossed Vidarh's face. "It's just a foolish notion. She has no interest in me...I'm not even sure if she thinks of me as a friend, she keeps her thoughts so close. I mean, at Gladsheim she was polite and friendly. She was never inhospitable or anything like that, but she didn't relax her guard with me, not for a moment. Even now, when I manage to contact her, she keeps her thoughts guarded."

Jess gave his shoulder a gentle squeeze. "Give her a little time, Vidarh, after all, you haven't known each other all that long. And this is a very difficult situation."

Vidarh stopped and raised his arm so his wrist flare illuminated the area before them. She saw an alcove, smaller than the one in which they had been imprisoned. A bundle of rags in one corner had presumably been a bed. He looked at Jess, and she read the anguish on his face.

"She's not here. I'm certain this is where she was."

"Then Hedrohan will have taken her with the others. It looks like she's taken them all."

Vidarh held out his hand. "Are you up to teleporting again?"

"Of course."

The teleportation seemed instantaneous this time, and Jess was beginning to get used to the sensation. Once back at the hopper, she sighed in frustration and despair. A heavy mist now covered the landscape, making the night seem even darker.

"We won't be able to see very far in this, even with the hopper's lights, and I'm not familiar with this territory. I don't want to delay going after Hedrohan, but it's too risky to go up in this."

"We can't be far behind her. I don't suppose she

can travel in the dark and mist any better than we can," Vidarh said. "It'll be a couple of hours before it starts to get light." He looked across at her. "We need to rest. I've lost track of when we last slept, but it was a long time ago. We haven't eaten, either."

Jess nodded wearily. "I *could* use a few hours of sleep. It won't do the others any good if we try to travel in the dark and I crash the hopper." She hesitated. "All our food packs, what's left of them, are hidden back in the forest. It's a bit late to go looking for them now, even if we could afford to deplete them even further—"

"Not to worry. If you build a fire, I'll see what I can catch. There should be a few nocturnal creatures around."

Vidarh climbed out from the hopper and adjusted his wrist flare. Within moments, he had disappeared into the mist and darkness. There were plenty of small branches and twigs lying around, and Jess soon gathered enough to make a small fire. She kept an alert eye out for any sign of danger, but it was unlikely the Salmarans would return. There was, after all, no reason for them to come back this way. They'd taken all the slaves.

In a remarkably short space of time, Vidarh returned, with two plump rodents, which he laid down beside the fire.

"That was quick," Jess said, trying not to wince as he expertly skinned and gutted the creatures. "How did you catch them in the mist?"

"I've had to hunt for my food all my life," he told her. "My hearing is so finely tuned now I can hear the animals and night birds in the forest before they know I'm there."

"It seems such a shame," Jess said, as he skewered the two carcasses onto a long branch and held it over the fire.

"I respect all forms of life, but it's the law of

nature. Sometimes we have to kill to survive. If it's any consolation I made it quick. They didn't have time to suffer."

When the animals were well-cooked, Vidarh carefully un-skewered them and sliced large chunks off both, dividing the meat into two portions.

Jess hesitated before she picked up her share. The smell of the meat seemed very strong, but Vidarh had obviously eaten these creatures before, and was already tucking into his meal with relish. They ate with their fingers, in silence, and although it tasted a little strange to her, the meat was certainly palatable.

Afterward, Jess rummaged in the back of the hopper and pulled out two thermal blankets. "These will keep us warm. We'd best damp down the fire and sleep in the hopper. It's a bit cramped, but it'll be warmer and safer than sleeping outside. You have the back, I'll take the front."

****

Jess awoke a few hours later, feeling light-headed and a little nauseous. Her limbs were stiff from sleeping in a confined position. She descended from the hopper, rubbed some fresh snow into her face in lieu of water, and began to revive a little. To her relief, the night mist had lifted and the sky was beginning to lighten. She was anxious to be on the move again, but Vidarh was already brewing kobah over a fresh fire and dishing out the leftover meat from the previous night's meal.

"Did you manage to get some sleep? You look a bit pale."

"I was so tired." Jess sat down and forced herself to eat some of the cold meat, which Vidarh had laid out on a large, clean leaf for a plate. It seemed to smell even stronger now, although she was sure many people would have found the aroma appetising, Vidarh was certainly tackling his own meal with great enthusiasm.

She had eaten only a few mouthfuls when, overcome with nausea, she fled from the campfire and lost her meagre breakfast behind a nearby clump of bushes.

She leaned against a tree trunk for a moment, feeling weak and a little dizzy. When she returned to the campsite, her overwhelming emotion was one of embarrassment.

"Are you all right?

"I'm sorry, I'm hardly ever ill. I don't know what brought it on."

"Sit here, by the fire." Vidarh placed a mug of steaming hot kobah in her hand. "Drink this, it'll help."

She blew on it, then took a few small sips. "Thanks. I'm starting to feel better now. I'm so sorry."

"I knew you should have taken a shot of that vaccine yourself. You'd better give yourself one from the stock in the hopper."

She forced a smile. "It's all right, Vidarh. It's not the sickness."

"How do you know? From all accounts, that's how it starts. Have you had any coughing...fever?"

She shook her head. "The broad-spectrum shots we have as a matter of routine will keep us immune. The vaccine is only a preventative anyway, not a cure, but it's not the sickness, please don't worry."

Vidarh was obviously not going to let the matter drop. "If it's not the sickness, then what?"

She looked at him with a wry smile. "I...I think it may have been the meat. You see, when you live on board a starship, eating flesh isn't practical. It's much more viable to grow plants for food, and I hate the thought of killing animals. I haven't eaten meat for years. I'm sorry, I suppose my system's just not used to it. Tamarith and her family are all vegetarians and I forgot that not everyone else is."

A look, which seemed to be a mixture of relief and deep remorse passed across Vidarh's face. "I should be the one apologising. I'm sorry. I never thought. I should've asked. That's the trouble with being raised as a farmer. It's part of our upbringing to go out and hunt something for supper."

Jess touched his arm. "I didn't want to make things difficult. I thought it would be all right. I didn't realize it would have this effect on me. I'm fine now though, really."

She saw him still looking at her, a slight frown creasing his brow, and she turned away to avoid his questioning gaze. In reality, she still felt pretty grim, but there was no point in worrying him any more.

"Promise me you'll see Hermot as soon as we get back to Gladsheim."

"It's all right," she said, rising to her feet. "I won't need to bother him. I'm sure it's just a reaction to eating flesh when I'm not used to it. I'll get our ship's computer to check me over, as soon as we get back. But do me a favour, though. Please don't tell Dahll...when we find him. He'll only worry, and that's the last thing he needs at the moment."

"All right, then. A promise for a promise. I'd like you to keep our little conversation yesterday to yourself. I would prefer no-one else knew how I feel about Tamarith."

"Of course. Now, back to the Salmarans. Their ferry must be closer than we thought for them to have got back to the caves so quickly."

"Perhaps they moved it closer when they realized there were more settlements here than on the Northern Continent," Vidarh suggested.

There was something in his voice, something more than the concern they both felt. Jess wondered what he was keeping from her. "What's up? Have you had any contact with Sleipnir today?

"Before you woke up." He hesitated. My father says several of the neighbouring homesteads have come down with the sickness. It's spreading again. Even if we stop the Salmarans, we may not be in time to save Sleipnir from the disease."

Chapter Eighteen

Vidarh busied himself clearing away the remains of the meal and damping down the fire.

"I wonder where Malmooth is?"

"I'll see if I can call him," Vidarh said. "He may come to me, if he's around." He closed his eyes in concentration, and a few minutes later they heard a low growl, and Malmooth appeared from the edge of the trees. He padded over to Jess.

"I'm glad to see you again, fella, I'd hate to have to explain to Tamarith that we'd lost her pet!"

"Do you think we ought to retrieve some of the food packs we hid?" Vidarh asked after a moment. "We might need them." He caught Jess in a yawn and, still feeling badly about the meat episode, added, "How about if you rest while I fetch them?"

She shook her head briskly. "Two of us will be able to carry more." Despite a few hours of sleep, Jess still looked tired but obviously had no intention of giving in to her lethargy. He tried not to notice her stifling another yawn as they trudged into the woods.

****

Three hours later, they spotted the Salmarans about ten kilometres away from Sleipnir. Vidarh had kept silent for the past hour or so, since Jess was obviously deep in thought, and he sensed she was also, uncharacteristically, in low spirits. His own mood had been far from optimistic, wondering if they had any chance of overcoming the Salmarans, and if his family would succumb to the sickness.

"Thank goodness," Jess breathed. "At least they

haven't reached the transporter ferry and loaded the prisoners." She adjusted the small scanner on the control panel in front of her, until the overlander was in focus. "They've stopped in the lee of those two low hills. There's someone getting out...it's Hedrohan and four other Salmarans, so it looks like they're only leaving one guard on board."

She eased the hopper to the ground and brought it to a halt. In one lithe movement, she leapt from her seat, Vidarh close behind. She went to the rear of the hopper and extracted several small, cylindrical objects.

"Good thing Dahll's so keen on playing around with explosives. He always said these would come in handy one day. They should cause some confusion, if nothing else."

Vidarh took two from her somewhat warily, with a wry grimace at the weight. Somehow, he hadn't expected them to be so heavy.

"Hold on." She disappeared into the back of the hopper again and reappeared with a number of hand blasters. "I'm not sure how many prisoners there are, but we can arm at least some of them." She stuck one in her belt and handed another to Vidarh. They divided the rest between them and stashed them in their packs.

"Let me have those other two mines," Vidarh said. "There's no point in carrying them when they're so heavy and there's an easier way," he told her. Moments later, all four objects were floating in the air a few metres in front of them.

"Telekinesis certainly has its uses," she remarked with a smile.

"I'll need to use energy to keep them moving," Vidarh said, "but it will be easier than toting them physically. Do we need to conceal the vehicle?" he asked.

"No, they'll know we're here soon enough and

with luck, by the time they do they won't be in any condition to cause any problems with the hopper. I'll fix up Dahll's anti-intrusion device, just in case, though."

When she finished activating the device, they made their way toward the Salmaran overlander, taking advantage of as much of the natural vegetation as possible for cover. They walked for roughly fifteen minutes before they saw the overlander in the distance.

Jess stopped and turned to Vidarh. "I think this is close enough. Can you make contact with Tamarith, yet?"

"I'll try." Vidarh slowly lowered the four mines to the ground, then closed his eyes and cast his thoughts toward Tamarith. Although it seemed more difficult than on previous occasions, at last, to his heartfelt relief, the tendrils of his mind touched hers.

Vidarh...Vidarh, I thought—I thought you'd lost us. Where are you?

Not far away—are you all right?

Yes...the Salmarans have all left, apart from a guard. From what I can make out, they're making for Sleipnir on foot. We're tied together and it's dark. We're going to try to release ourselves telekinetically but it will take some time.

How is Dahll?

He's alive, although he's lost a lot of blood. But he's stable. Please tell Jess.

He turned to Jess, and once more raised the mines into the air. "They're okay. The slavers have left them, and headed for Sleipnir. Dahll's holding his own."

"Thanks be," Jess said with feeling. "I won't be happy until I see him again though, and the others."

As soon as they reached the overlander, Jess checked the main hatch. "You'd better tell everyone inside to stand as far down one end as possible...well away from the hatch."

Vidarh nodded, once more placing the explosive devices on the ground, and stood with one hand on the vehicle's hull, his eyes closed in concentration, while Jess fixed two of the mines and adjusted the settings.

"Quick," she said, "down behind that rock. It's primed to go off in twenty seconds."

They dived for cover behind the boulder Jess indicated, and Vidarh threw himself down beside her.

A muffled explosion shook the ground, followed by a small cloud of dark smoke.

"Just hope Hedrohan didn't hear that or she may come back to investigate," Jess said as they raised their heads above the rock.

"It wasn't particularly loud," Vidarh said, with some surprise.

"There're not really very powerful. Enough to break open the hatch, though." They were both on their feet, and running toward the transporter. The former captives were already descending to the ground through the gaping hole that had once been an entry hatch.

Vidarh did a quick count and deduced there were about twelve of them. He strained his eyes, looking for one person in particular. Then he saw her, helping Melind alight to the ground. He quelled the impulse to rush over to her, shielding his thoughts. She mustn't know how concerned he had been about her. Not yet, anyway. Not until he had an opportunity to speak to her alone and find out if there was a chance she could feel anything for him.

What's happened to the Salmaran who was guarding you? he telepathed instead.

Tamarith stopped to pet Malmooth, who had gone bounding up to her, and gazed across at him.

He seems to have become suddenly very drowsy...some of us thought he needed a nap.

The effects of whatever Hedrohan had drugged them with had obviously worn off, and although Nifls were reluctant to use their telepathic powers as a weapon, in this case the group of prisoners had decided it was necessary. Hedrohan, it seemed, had underestimated the power of the Nifl mind.

Thank you, Vidarh. If it wasn't for you and Jess...

Her words in his mind trailed off. Her face looked pale and drawn. A livid bruise showed black and purple against the alabaster whiteness of her skin. He flashed her a quick smile in response, then turned away quickly, to hide the anger he felt rising up inside him. Whatever it took, he would track Hedrohan down and make the slave leader pay for what she had done to Tamarith.

He looked back toward the overlander, as Dahll came down the ramp, supported by Gullin. Jess ran to him and threw her arms around him. They held each other for several moments, palpably relieved at seeing each other again. With Gullin holding on to Dahll's good arm to steady him, they walked together to where Vidarh stood.

"It's a good thing you and Jess got here when you did," Dahll said, his face pale, but otherwise looking in better shape than Vidarh had expected. He winced slightly as Jess helped him remove his thermal outer garment, and carefully unwrapped the makeshift bandage.

"Who dressed your wounds?" she asked.

"One of the Salmarans. They were obviously afraid I might bleed to death and lower their profits."

"Lucky you were wearing this suit when you were shot, or the damage might have been worse," Jess observed, frowning. She put down her pack and withdrew one of the bio-regenerators, which she ran over Dahll's shoulder and chest.

Vidarh heard her sigh of relief as he watched.

"It's working." She looked back at Dahll. "It'll take a while for your body to replace the blood you've lost, but the healing process is almost completed, it was deep and nasty, but it didn't damage the bone."

"Thanks, sweetheart," Dahll said, shrugging back into his thermal jacket, and tucking the bio-regenerator, which Jess had handed him, into his pocket. He already looked stronger.

Jess began to administer the anti-serum to the recently rescued captives.

"Soon as you've finished, we'd better get after Hedrohan," Dahll said. "It seems likely she's making for Sleipnir."

Jess shook her head. "Not until you've rested. You need to make up that blood loss—"

"I'm fine. I've had a lot worse things happen to me. I'll rest here while you finish the vaccinations."

"You're going to need a while longer than that to recover...a few hours at least."

"We don't have a few hours. We have to stop Hedrohan before she reaches Sleipnir. How are the others? What about Melind?"

"I'm fine, so's everyone else." Melind had come up behind Jess, who shook her head at Dahll in exasperation.

"Then let's not hang around here," Tamarith said. Her gaze lingered on Dahll a moment, and Vidarh did not miss her expression of concern. "Jess and Dahll can stay here while he recovers. With luck we'll get there before the fighting gets underway."

Vidarh stared at Tamarith in surprise. It wasn't just the vehemence with which she had spoken the words. He'd seen a fleeting, tantalising glimpse of her mind as well, just for an instant, and he realized that this lovely, seemingly gentle woman was capable of hatred. He wondered what Hedrohan had forced her and the others to endure. She might have relaxed her mind for a moment, just enough to allow him to sense her anger, but he knew her well enough by now to be sure she would keep whatever she had gone through carefully shielded.

Dahll stood, a little unsteadily, grasping his blaster with determination. "You won't leave me," he said, "you're going to need everyone capable of handling a weapon if you want to protect Sleipnir against Salmarans."

****

"Wish we still had the ponies," Melind panted, trying to keep up with Gullin.

"Is your ankle hurting you?" he asked, taking her arm.

"No, it's just that we'd catch up with the Salmarans quicker than on foot."

"We've a better chance of taking them by surprise without the ponies," Dahll said.

The land became more level and open as they approached Sleipnir. A thin covering of snow still covered the grassland, and herd animals grazed on the short grass beneath. The trees had thinned out and the group hugged the base of the low-lying hills. Vidarh, at the head of the little band, kept the remaining two mines hovering, and checked the turquoise, cloudless sky. There was no hint of the contrary, unpredictable mist.

Eventually he stopped and raised a hand. The others crept up behind him and followed his gaze. They stood on a low outcrop of rock, and there, spread below them in the distance, lay the little hamlet of Sleipnir. Large rocks and boulders littered the clearing below them and the land supported no vegetation except for a few skeletal trees. The figures of Hedrohan and her band, obviously intent on taking the settlement by surprise, could be seen skirting the mountains to the west.

"If you can, send a message to Sleipnir," Dahll said, "to warn them." He glanced at Jess. "We can fool Hedrohan into thinking there are more of us than there actually are."

She nodded, catching his meaning. "Vidarh, let's have the other two explosives."

When they floated gently to the ground, Dahll picked them up and adjusted the settings. "I've set them as high as they'll go—they're only likely to do real damage at close range. The propulsion units probably won't last long enough to get them that close, but they'll give off a fair bit of smoke."

He placed the mines on the edge of the slope. On their own power now, they skimmed down the rock face, then hovered across the grassland to land some distance behind the group of Salmarans. As the first explosive detonated, a brilliant light flared for a moment and a dull roar reverberated back from the mountains. A wall of black smoke obscured the suns as the Nifls, with Jess and Dahll following at a slower pace, ran down the incline toward the surprised Salmarans, firing their blasters as they went.

Chapter Nineteen

The landscape filled with noise and confusion. As the second device went off, the Salmarans scattered and ran toward the nearest cover. The moment Vidarh reached the bottom of the shallow incline, he threw himself behind a large boulder. He raised his weapon and ducked down again as a volley of blaster fire sent shards of shattered rock flying past him. Shielding his eyes from the fragments and the vivid flash, he risked a glance sideways, noting with relief that the others had also flattened themselves behind several of the large boulders.

Few Nifls were used to fighting, or using an energy weapon. Vidarh was probably the best equipped for combat, being accustomed to the use of weapons when hunting for food, or protecting the herd animals from predators.

Even so, shooting at humanoid beings was a different matter. He aimed the unfamiliar, high-velocity power weapon at the rocks behind which the Salmarans had retreated, ducking instinctively as his fire elicited a response. A flaming tongue of purple energy from his opponent only just missing his head. He felt the heat of its passage while the air around shifted and shimmered with an intensity that almost blinded him.

Vidarh fired again, rewarded by a horrific screech as the energy bolt hit home. For several minutes, the air was ablaze with blaster fire and the lethal whining of blasters. Hoarse shouts reached his ear and he assumed some of the shots had found their targets. It was impossible to tell how badly injured their opponents were, or whether any of his companions had been hit. He was so occupied with the task of staying alive himself he had no opportunity to cast his mind to find out.

After a while, the residue of smoke from the explosives and the stench of burning flesh made his eyes sting. He blinked to try to ease his vision and a Salmaran came out of nowhere, lunging at him with a snarl like a crazed animal, and knocked Vidarh off his feet.

He rolled out of the way and stood again. Hand-to-hand combat was more familiar to him, and Vidarh felt more in control. The Salmaran was taller and heavier than he, but unarmed—no doubt the alien's weapon had exhausted its charge.

Vidarh landed a hefty punch to the Salmaran's jaw. His opponent rocked back on his heels, then swung at Vidarh's head. Vidarh ducked and threw all his weight behind another blow.

This time the Salmaran went down, and stayed down.

Vidarh retrieved his weapon from where it had fallen and dived behind the nearest rock to avoid another deadly beam of blaster fire. He peered out from behind his cover. The Salmaran he had just fought was obviously not the only one to have broken cover, and through the smoke haze, he saw several of his companions struggling furiously with their Salmaran opponents.

He sensed, rather than heard, a slight movement behind him, and whirled around to confront another of the slavers. He ducked out of the way, firing at the same time, and had the satisfaction of seeing the man fall backward.

A sudden force pushed Vidarh sideways. He felt a burning sensation in his arm and realized he had been hit by blaster fire from behind. The energy bolt had torn through the thick hide of his coat and blood seeped through the leather, although the garment had probably saved him from far greater injury.

He flung himself to the ground and turned to shoot back at the Salmaran. His aim was accurate, his hunting experience standing him in good stead. The Salmaran shrieked and threw up his arms, before falling to the ground.

The air grew even thicker with smoke and the smell of burning, and blaster fumes. He tried to make out how many Salmarans were still on their feet. It seemed they might have underestimated the slavers' numbers. The firing appeared to have ceased for the moment, but he ducked down behind a rock again while he strained his mind, trying to reach the others, to discern if any were injured. He touched the minds of Melind and Gullin. They at least seemed to have escaped injury.

Tamarith! Where was she? He was about to transmit the question when he felt another energy blast to his left. He risked a peek over the rock. Dahll and Jess were both sheltered behind a nearby outcrop, and he heard a yell as one of them aimed and hit their target. How many Salmarans were left?

All at once, the battlefield became deathly quiet. Were the Salmarans defeated, or was this a trick to put the Nifls off guard? Where *was* Tamarith?

After several minutes without any further gunfire, cautiously Vidarh raised himself up and looked around. The smoke had dissipated a little and he was relieved to see Gullin and Melind easing their way in his direction.

His arm was starting to throb and pain seared through him. His eyes still smarted from the acrid smoke and for a moment his senses drifted and the earth beneath his feet seemed to spin, causing him to stagger and sway unsteadily.

He fought to regain his equilibrium and abruptly experienced a moment of confusion. Myriad colours flashed before his eyes as a vision of Tamarith—and another figure, Hedrohan—tore his thoughts apart. They were not in the area where the recent melee had taken place. Tamarith was dodging, ducking down behind any available cover to avoid Hedrohan's fire. Vidarh's blood chilled as he realized they were headed toward the ravine known as Loki's Chasm.

He caught Gullin's realisation of the danger she was in, and telepathed reassurance. *I know, Gullin. Don't worry, I am familiar with the terrain.*

He visualised the area near the chasm, where he had spent hours hunting as a boy, and pictured the inhospitable territory and the dark ravine as the two combatants drew closer to the edge. The fear he felt for Tamarith banished Vidarh's former feelings of weakness and vertigo. He bent low, running behind the rocks for cover as he made for Loki's Chasm.

He ignored the pain in his arm, straining to see through the murk of dust and smoke as he stumbled over Salmaran bodies in the haze. He heard the unmistakable whine and zing of blasters up ahead, and realized the battle raged on.

When he reached the antagonists, they had both thrown down their weapons, charges presumably spent. They crouched, circling each other warily. Hedrohan wielded a strangely designed dagger and Tamarith held a similar knife, taken, Vidarh assumed, from one of the dead Salmarans lying nearby.

They fought perilously close to the chasm that yawned before them. The Salmaran might be far superior in height and build to Tamarith, but the young Nifl woman was more agile. Hedrohan slashed at Tamarith repeatedly with the heavy dagger and each time Tamarith ducked. So far she was avoiding injury but Vidarh did not think she could be very experienced when it came to knife fighting. Nor would she be at full strength after her ordeal.

Vidarh dared not show himself or transmit a message to Tamarith for fear of distracting her. He eyed a nearby rock, intending to use his powers of levitation to aim it at the slaver. Before he could put his thoughts into action, he sensed figures behind him. He turned to see Dahll darting for cover closely followed by Melind. All at once, he sensed the distress emanating from Melind and reproached himself for not realising something was terribly wrong. He'd been concentrating so much on Tamarith he'd all but forgotten about Melind's feelings for him.

Perhaps he should have stayed and fought with his friends. Tamarith seemed to be far more capable of defending herself than he gave her credit for. She obviously did not need his help.

Where are Gullin...and Jess?

Gullin has been hurt...badly. Jess is tending to him, Melind telepathed. He could sense she was scared and it occurred to him she had only now realized that what she'd thought of as an exciting adventure was far more dangerous.

He sent her swift, reassuring vibes, telling her Gullin would be fine, to remember that Jess had Phidian medicaments and instruments to deal with his injuries. He hoped he was right. After all, he did not know how badly Gullin's wounds were, and he supposed even Jess could not perform miracles.

He turned his attention back to Tamarith and Hedrohan just as the Salmaran woman lunged at Tamarith and grasped her knife hand. As she raised her other arm to strike, Vidarh saw his chance, aimed his blaster and squeezed the trigger button, holding his breath.

Hedrohan yelled and dropped the knife, clutching her shoulder and shoving Tamarith to the ground at the edge of the ravine, where she fell heavily, hitting her head on the rocky surface.

Vidarh's heart lurched in his chest, terrified Tamarith might be seriously injured He squeezed the trigger once more but to his dismay, there was no response. It needed time to recharge. He lunged at Hedrohan, who brought her arm up and caught him with a heavy backhand, felling him to the ground.

She reached down and retrieved her dagger, then turned to face Dahll, her eyes cold as the depths of the chasm behind her. As Vidarh rose cautiously to his feet, he felt a chill run through him. The hate and malice this alien woman projected was something he had never experienced before—but it was not directed at him.

"So, Dahll Tarron," she snarled, ignoring Vidarh and Melind. It seems I should've killed you when I had the opportunity."

"Whatever quarrel you have with me," Dahll said, looking pale, but standing firm with his blaster aimed directly at Hedrohan's head, "it has nothing to do with these three. Let them go."

The woman's eyes became dark slits. "You would negotiate...with me?" Her tone of contempt implied she was in control of the situation, even though Dahll appeared to have the upper hand.

Dahll made a threatening gesture with his gun. "I wasn't thinking of negotiation—"

"Murderer! Word of your deeds has reached Salmar. You are the coward who killed my kinsman, one of Salmar's greatest heroes, on the planet Lyrrh. The legend is told among our people of how, single-handed, he fought an entire ship's crew led by the Anraatian, Dahll Tarron, who shot him in the back. I will be the one to bring you back to atone for your cowardly deeds." She nodded toward Vidarh and Melind. "And there is my bonus. Your friends will bring a good price as slaves."

Vidarh could not imagine the Anraatian committing murder, but Dahll merely smiled.

"I reckon history gets distorted on all worlds. As for taking slaves, you might as well forget any more slave hunting on Niflheim...don't you know its people are inflicted with a disease that threatens to become pandemic?"

To Vidarh's amazement, the woman began to laugh, a raucous sound that echoed across the barren mountains.

"You fools. Have you not yet realized?"

Dahll's face registered sudden comprehension. "It was you? Why? Sick slaves won't be much use—"

"Fool! The disease was supposed to have no lasting ill effects, just to suppress their telepathic powers, so I could take the inhabitants of this planet by surprise."

"I should kill you now," Dahll told her, his voice heavy with contempt. "But I need to know how to get past the forcefield that prevents us from leaving this planet. If you tell me I might allow you to live, and let the people of Niflheim decide what's to be done with you."

"What forcefield? I know nothing of any forcefield."

"You're lying. Tell me—now!"

Dahll steadied his aim with purpose, but Hedrohan only laughed.

"Believe what you like. You won't shoot me. Not in cold blood."

Without warning, she scooped up Tamarith's limp form and held the young woman in front of her, the knife directed at Tamarith's throat. "And I doubt you'll risk the life of this girl."

Before any of them could react, there was a

horrific howl and a large, cream-colored form leapt at the Salmaran woman. The animal's cry of outrage rent the air as, flinging Tamarith aside, Hedrohan screamed and fell backward onto the ground, with Malmooth on top of her.

Vidarh watched in frozen horror as Tamarith's body sailed into the air and over the edge of the ravine, into the chasm below.

Melind screamed and ran to the edge of the chasm, her mind crying out to him in anguish.

In that instant, Vidarh knew what he had to do.

Steeling himself, and blocking his mind to everything except Tamarith, ran forward and flung himself over the edge.

Chapter Twenty

The speed of his fall shocked Vidarh's mind into action. He willed himself to stabilise his descent, to drop feet first into the void. He had no idea if the chasm really was bottomless—logic told him there had to be some floor to the ravine. It couldn't just go on forever. There was, most likely, a river at the bottom, although no one who had fallen into the abyss had ever returned to confirm whether or not this was the case.

The sides of the chasm appeared to close in toward him, as he inhaled the cold, dank air. The mist itself seemed to have invaded the crevasse, its freezing dampness touching his face like the deceitful caress of something black and malevolent, smelling of rot and decay.

He sensed, rather than saw, sharp, twisted spikes of rock reaching out as if to tear him to pieces, and he could only hope Tamarith would avoid their evil barbs.

Tamarith, can you hear me? There was no answer, but he felt her presence below him, and he perceived a mingling of terror and despair. She was conscious now, but made no attempt to save herself.

Tamarith. I'm here with you. Slow yourself down. You can do it, just use your mind as if you were levitating.

Still nothing. He pushed aside his scruples, the edict of non-intrusion instilled into all Nifls, and in desperation, reached into her mind with his.

He was shocked at the feelings of hurt and despair and that enveloped him. She did not care what happened to her or that she was hurtling to her death. She believed Gullin was unlikely to survive his injuries. Dahll would never think of her as anything other than a friend, and she had nothing to live for.

Dahll?

Vidarh withdrew just enough to retain contact, without probing any deeper into her secret thoughts. He used his willpower to control the speed of his descent, while maintaining the tenuous touching of their minds. *Tamarith...please, listen to me. Don't you realize how many people care for you, need you? Your family needs you...your friends. Gullin...he still lives. He needs you.*

Was he mistaken or did he feel a spark, a tiny part of her mind reaching back to him? Carefully accelerating his descent again, he sent down invisible strands of thought, trying to harness her consciousness to his own. *Please Tamarith. Please save yourself. You're not alone. Tamarith....don't leave me.* Still she would not open her mind enough to join fully with his, to listen to him and know what he said was true. The despair that gripped his heart tore the words from his mind.

Tamarith...I love you!

That hit home. A tangle of emotions washed over him, disbelief, shock, confusion. He was close now, less than a metre above her. He felt her in the darkness, turning toward him. He could almost reach out and touch her. How much further did they have to fall? At any moment they might hit the rocks below, or be drowned in the river that must have carved the abyss. He could still lose her.

Tamarith, let me take your hands. In the pitch-blackness, he focussed all his powers of telepathy on his beloved. He could sense her as clearly as if he could see her. He angled his body so that he was directly in front of her, and reached out...and at last, touched her fingers. He clasped them tightly in his own, and unseen lightning sparked though his body, sending his mind reeling so he almost lost his concentration.

Open your mind. Visualise the ground above us...now! The melding of their minds, when it happened, was like a power shock. This was different from how it had been with Jess. Her mind had been receptive, malleable, with a great deal of potential for training, but Tamarith's was already powerful...as powerful as he now knew his own to be, although she did not realize it yet. Only part of her mind was open to him, like a shaft of light through a partly opened door, but it was enough.

He had a brief mental picture of the silver strands that bound her to her siblings. Strands like silk, as fine as those of a spider's web, but infinitely stronger. One reached out, connecting to another person, not of their world.

To Dahll Tarron.

Vidarh's heart sank, but this strand was tenuous, growing weaker as it reached away from her, although she still held it in her mind. Immediately he put the image to one side and focussed on the land bordering one side of the chasm. Fiercely he projected the likeness into Tamarith's head, blotting out every other thought and propelling them both upward with his mind.

His will and his intent focussed on one thing only, teleporting them both to safety, while avoiding the treacherous barbs on each side of the ravine. A rainbow flash of intense light filled him with an almost unbearable radiance. His concentration was such that a physical pain throbbed behind his eyes and his lungs strained. His heart pounded in his chest. The terrain at the edge of the chasm was sharply defined now. He pictured its every detail and could almost feel it beneath his feet. A sudden blackness, a swirling, biting rush of cold, the blackness changed to whirling colours. Then he stood on firm ground once more, Tamarith in front of him, her hands still in his.

He took a deep breath as he released her. For a moment she stared into his eyes, a look of amazement on her face as her mind withdrew from his.

How...how did you do that?

She had asked him the same question at their first meeting. It seemed like a lifetime ago.

I didn't, you did it yourself...or rather, we did it together. He hesitated, recalling how he had forced his mind into hers, something that was not only unpardonable, but was usually impossible except between very close relatives or loved ones. *I'm sorry about—*

She lowered her eyes and dropped her head, hiding her expression. *Don't worry, I know you only said what you said to get my attention...to make me come to my senses, I won't hold you to it.*

Vidarh frowned. That was not what he had meant. She looked up again and his glance went to those beautiful, unfathomable dark eyes, which he now realized were not black, nor even midnight blue, but deepest violet. He tried to summon the courage to tell her what he really felt—that he had meant it when he told her he loved her.

The moment was shattered when Melind, tears coursing down her face, ran toward them and threw her arms around her sister.

"Thank goodness Vidarh saved you. I thought I'd lost you. And Gullin's injured, badly. Jess is tending to him. Malmooth's hurt too—but Dahll took care of him." Vidarh saw the look of shock on Tamarith's face and wished Melind hadn't blurted out all the bad news quite so bluntly.

Before he could speak to Tamarith again, Dahll

appeared, and flashed Vidarh an admiring look. "Don't know how you did that, but I was afraid you'd both plunged to your deaths."

"How long ago was it?" Vidarh asked, "It seemed like hours, but it's still light."

"It all happened in the space of a few minutes," Dahll told him. We had no idea what was happening down there."

"How is Gullin? Tamarith asked anxiously. "Will...will he recover?"

"I can't say for sure, but Jess is a good healer, if anyone can save him, she can."

He closed his eyes for a moment, leaning against one of the few trees, and Vidarh noticed the unusual pallor of his face.

"Are you all right?"

Dahll nodded. "Yes, still a bit weak, though."

"Jess was right. You should have rested rather than fight so soon without giving your body a chance to recover."

Dahll gave him a slow grin. "You don't have much room to talk. You're bleeding."

Vidarh had almost forgotten his own injury. As he became aware of the pain and the dried blood caking the tattered remnants of his sleeve, he had a sudden thought. "What happened to Hedrohan?"

"She got away." Dahll's expression was grim. "We were so concerned with what was happening to you and Tamarith—"

"It's my fault she got away," Melind confessed. "Dahll was going to go after her, but I asked him not to leave me alone. I'm sorry."

"It's all right," Dahll said, putting a consoling arm around the girl. "There's still enough light to follow her. She's on foot and injured. It won't take me long to catch up with her."

"No," Vidarh said, "I'll go after her. She's caused the deaths of countless people of Niflheim. I want revenge."

"But you're hurt," Dahll objected.

"So are you. I'll be all right."

"My wound's nearly healed."

"You're still weak from loss of blood. Besides," Vidarh directed Dahll's glance toward the first range of the Hela Mountains into which Hedrohan had disappeared. "I know those peaks. They're dangerous for anyone not familiar with them."

"We'll go together. You don't know what you're up against. You're not used to fighting, although I have to admit you handled yourself pretty well back there."

"I'll be quicker alone. Sleipnir's not like Gladsheim, there are renegades and rustlers who hide out in the mountains. I've had to defend our herds on more than one occasion. I'm more used to fighting than you imagine."

He drew Dahll a short distance away from Tamarith and Melind and lowered his voice. "Please...stay with them, there could still be Salmarans around. I want to do this...I *need* to do it. For Tamarith and what that woman put her through."

The two men locked gazes, then, abruptly, Dahll relented.

"I can relate to that." For a moment his face had a faraway look, as if remembering something. "All right, I'll stay here and keep watch over Malmooth with Tamarith and Melind, until he's recovered enough for us to go back to the others." His gaze went to Vidarh's sleeve, encrusted with dried blood. "I won't argue with your right to kill Hedrohan, but let me see to your arm first."

Vidarh removed his coat and allowed Dahll to run the bio-regenerator over his wound. When he finished, Vidarh flexed the arm several times before putting his coat back on.

"It's amazing. It hardly feels as if I was injured at all."

"We're lucky the Salmarans are mainly using blasters," Dahll said. If they had lasers, you'd have lost that arm and a bio-regenerator wouldn't have been able to restore it. On the other hand, if you'd been closer and taken the full force of the blaster fire there wouldn't be anything of you left to heal."

Vidarh grinned. "How reassuring." He nodded toward Melind and Tamarith. "I know neither of them think they need looking after, but Melind is distraught with worry and Tamarith has been through so much—"

"Don't worry, I'll watch out for them. But take care, Hedrohan may be wounded but that will make her more dangerous. I've dealt with Salmarans before. As a race, they're completely ruthless." He paused. "How about a bio-regenerator?"

"I've got one," Vidarh said, patting his hip pocket. He turned toward the mountains. "I'd best try to make up some ground before nightfall."

As Dahll turned back, Vidarh heard a voice in his mind.

Vidarh, what's going on?

There's something I have to do. Don't worry about me. Melind. I'll be all right.

You're going after Hedrohan, aren't you? I'm coming with you.

No! The command was sharper than he'd intended, but the last thing he needed was a teenage girl tagging along, especially when all he could think of at the moment was her sister.

Melind, I can't afford to have anyone with me.

Please. I can help.

Help get me killed? Stay with Tamarith, she's suffered more than you seem to realise. She doesn't need anything more to have to cope with.

He hadn't meant to hurt her but he felt her

distress as the retort came back.

That's it isn't it? You're in love with my sister. You never had any feelings for me at all. It was her all the time!

There was no point in denying it. Anything he tried to say would only hurt her more. Pursing his lips, he closed his mind, shutting off her protests. She would be safe with the others. That was what mattered.

He took a long, lingering look toward Tamarith, bent over the wounded icecat, with Melind standing a short way off, glaring at him. A longing came over him to walk back over to Tamarith. To take her in his arms and tell her how much he loved her.

To ask her to wait for his return...if he returned.

He drew a deep breath. Tamarith did not care for him.

Her heart belonged to Dahll.

Chapter Twenty-One

Tamarith looked up at Dahll's approach, and realized, too late, that Vidarh had left.

Her mind whirled in confusion. Vidarh had saved her life, and she had not even thanked him. Her cheeks burned as she remembered the words he'd sent into her mind, the tingling in her fingers when his strong hands had held them. She swallowed, hard.

Of course, he had not meant it. He'd obviously felt a declaration of love was the only way he could reach her.

Well, he was right about that. She had been so miserable and self-pitying, so stubborn.

But Tamarith could not get Vidarh's face out of her mind, the expression of sadness in those hazel eyes, eyes that in a certain light shone almost golden. In the time she had been Hedrohan's captive, Vidarh had been the only one who was able to keep in contact with her. When minds touched as theirs had, it was impossible not to gain some insight into a person's deepest self, and there was a lot about Vidarh to admire...and to like.

She let out her breath in a long sigh. She could no longer deny that what she felt for Vidarh was far more than liking or admiration.

And now he was going into danger.

Alone.

Her heart thudded painfully in her chest. What if he did not return? What if she never saw him again?

She stood and looked in the direction of the Hela

Mountains where Vidarh's figure, dark against the snow, grew ever smaller. "You go on, Dahll, take Melind back to where you left Jess and the others. I'm going after Vidarh."

Dahll laid a hand on Tamarith's arm. "You're not going anywhere. You hit your head. You might be suffering the effects of a concussion."

She tried to contain her impatience while he parted her hair with his hand, and then ran the bio-regenerator over her head.

"It looks all right and should heal fine. But you'd better get some rest."

"I'm going after Vidarh." It seemed impossible that she was so close to Dahll and he seemed to have no effect on her. All she could think of now was Vidarh.

"Tamarith, Vidarh wants to do this alone, and I can understand why. He knows the mountains in this area. None of *us* do. He didn't want me to go with him, and if he senses you're following him he may worry about you and get careless."

"But what if he gets hurt? I can't let him face her alone."

Dahll's expression as he shook his head left Tamarith in no doubt he would do anything he could to stop her from following Vidarh. "I don't like it either, but he insisted. We have to respect his wishes. You'll know if he's in trouble, won't you?"

Tamarith nodded, biting her lip. "Yes, but it may be too late by then."

"Look," Dahll said, lightly touching her shoulder, "We need to get back to Jess and Gullin. Later you can send a message to Vidarh, and if he seems to be in any danger I'll go back after him, myself." He glanced at Melind. "Your sister's not coping with all of this too well," Dahll said in a low voice. "She'll be even more upset if you put yourself in danger again—and Gullin needs to see you, too."

Tamarith set her mouth in a firm line. What Dahll said made sense. It seemed she had no alternative, for the moment, but she kept her mind open, hoping against hope Vidarh would make contact.

When they returned to the area where Dahll had left Jess, Gullin, and the rest of the wounded, Tamarith gasped at the sight of the bodies littered on the rocky floor of the valley, then hastily turned aside. At least most of her fellow prisoners seemed to have survived. Several, with bandaged arms and legs, stood or sat near to where Jess was tending Gullin.

As soon as she saw Dahll, Jess, her cheeks visibly paling, ran over to her lifemate, gesturing him to sit down. From a small flask taken from her pack, she poured a concoction and stood protectively over him while he drank it.

Tamarith hurried over to where her brother lay covered in a thermal blanket.

"Don't worry," Jess said, coming up behind Tamarith, "I've done everything I can for him, and I think he's going to be all right. He'll sleep for a while, now. I've just given Dahll something to make him sleep, too, to give him chance to recuperate. He'll be out for a long time. I think you should rest, as well."

"I'm all right," Tamarith replied, planting a soft kiss on Gullin's brow, her mind wandering to the mountains beyond Loki's Chasm. How was Vidarh faring? Would he be able to defeat Hedrohan?

She repeatedly sent her thoughts to him, but she could not make contact. Perhaps he'd closed his mind to enable him to concentrate on going after the Salmaran. Tamarith would not allow herself to think of the alternative. She could only hope he would make contact if he was in trouble...and they would be able to reach him in time.

At Jess's insistence, Tamarith ate some of the food from their packs. Then she wrapped a blanket around herself and lay down by the campfire, just outside the shelter Jess had rigged. She stayed awake for what seemed like several hours, trying to vanquish the jumbled thoughts from her mind. Every time she closed her eyes and tried to sleep, she saw Vidarh's face, his eyes—the crooked little smile he had when he was thinking.

Why had he gone after the Salmaran woman alone?

She tried to relax, and when at last sleep came to her, she dreamed...

The air was quiet. Nothing disturbed the silence. Tamarith ceased her endless climbing and listened. All at once, the sound of rocks falling down the mountainside shattered the stillness. She shrank against the cliff, her feet giving way beneath her. Just as she thought she would lose her footing completely, she found herself floating.

The blackness surrounded her. She was alone in the dark. The walls of her prison closed in and she was falling now, falling into interminable nothingness, the nothingness of Loki's Chasm. A voice called out to her, but she could not comprehend the words. Usually telepathic communication did not even need words for the meaning to be understood. The blackness melted into the blinding white of snow.

Snow and mist, nothing but snow and mist. A huge shadowy shape towered over her. Black. Evil. All at once, the air scintillated purple and green, the stars tilted in the heavens and the ground crumbled beneath her. Pain filled her body as a flaming sword sliced through skin, sinew, muscle. Blood seeped in a scarlet tide into the snow. With one last effort, she raised her knife to strike a blow at the apparition's heart, its face shifted and distorted. For a moment she saw, quite clearly, the Salmaran slaver.

Then she gazed into a pale, lifeless face, which no longer resembled Hedrohan. Golden eyes, dark auburn hair...

Vidarh!

Tamarith jerked upright, staring wide-eyed into the gloom, wondering if she had really spoken his name aloud or just imagined she had. She was shaking with apprehension, convinced something terrible had happened to the man she had grown to love. She shook her head. What was the matter with her? She'd had a nightmare, that was all.

But it had been so vivid, more like a vision, a prescience even.

She threw off her blankets, and, picking up her travel pack, crept from the makeshift camp. She took care not to disturb Jess, who had fallen asleep in a sitting position, her blaster across her knees. Tamarith smiled in the moonlight, aware the other woman had been awake while the others slept, keeping watch.

Tamarith inched past her on tiptoe, knowing Jess was a light sleeper. Jess had said she would not close her eyes until she was sure there were no Salmarans still in the area. She had to be exhausted.

Melind slept soundly, as did Gullin and Dahll, who was presumably still under the influence of the draught Jess had given him. Tamarith knew her sister and Gullin would be safe and well looked after. She'd telepath a message to Melind when it was daylight. By then she'd be too far away for anyone to come after her.

Tamarith could no longer ignore the icy fear that gripped her heart, the feeling Vidarh was in trouble. He might not want her heart, but she owed him her life and it was payback time.

She tucked her blaster in her belt and looked toward the mountains.

Welcome or not, she had to follow him.

****

Vidarh's mind was a farrago of emotions. Part of him reached out to the settlement of Sleipnir. It had been some time since he had last communicated with his kinsfolk and he feared the worst. Something was very wrong, or surely the villagers would have joined in the fight against the Salmarans. Why could he not make contact with them? He was worried the sickness had already struck. There could be no other reason for his inability to reach them.

Another portion of his mind wrestled with the truth of what, in his desperation to get through to her, he had revealed to Tamarith. The love he had hitherto tried to hide, although Jess had guessed it. How could Tamarith not have realized he meant what he said?

He was almost relieved she did not believe him. Their minds had not just touched, they had merged. He had seen the ties that bound her to Dahll, although they were weakening. She knew Dahll would never love any woman except Jess, but Vidarh had not been able to detect any feelings for himself, either.

Even if he had been tempted to probe more deeply, there was no time, their combined mental powers barely sufficient to teleport them from the depths of the abyss to safety.

He tried to concentrate on his pursuit of Hedrohan and close his mind to everything else. The mist descended again and frequent flurries of snow stung his face, causing him to pull his hood more closely over his head. Darkness fell fast and the mist obscured the moon that struggled to escape from behind the clouds.

He knew in a short time darkness would completely cover the land. The tortuous, zigzagging track did not make his pursuit of Hedrohan easy.

It was fortunate he understood these mountains so well. He had grown to manhood in their shadow, and hunted beneath their baleful gaze.

As he climbed higher, the snow flurries became heavier and a spiteful wind howled and tugged at his coat. He paused to rest for a while. The effort of teleporting had drained much of his energy, and he knew he still suffered the effects of blood loss. He would need all his wits and cunning to defeat Hedrohan. Vidarh took a deep draught of water and replaced the bottle in his pack, studying the mountain above him. There was still a long way to go before he reached the summit.

He laboured along the steep, almost non-existent goat-track for several more minutes, until it eventually petered out altogether. He prepared himself for the difficult climb to the top.

All at once, he halted. Hedrohan was not far away. He could not see her, or even hear her, but he sensed her presence.

His intuition was well-founded. Moments later a boulder came rattling past his head, sending several small stones and pebbles clattering down the mountainside.

So, Hedrohan had resorted to throwing rocks. Did that mean her weapon had still not recharged?

The answer came almost immediately, as a burst of purple flame flashed above him, lighting up the mountainside, and a small landslide nearly knocked him off his feet and down the almost sheer face of the cliff. He reached out in desperation, while trying to regain a foothold in the sliding scree, his fingers clutching at a spindly tree growing out of the bare rock.

To his relief it held.

Vidarh dug his feet into the rock and hollowed his back. He tucked his head down into his chest and pressed against the cliff wall to protect himself as much as possible from the rocks and debris, which together with huge chunks of ice, rushed past and over him with a sound like thunder. Even so, he felt glancing blows from some of them. Dirt and dust mingled with the falling snow, and he coughed and spluttered, fighting for breath.

When the clatter of gravel and small stones finally ceased, he risked raising his head to look around. His ears still rang from the noise of the avalanche, and he caught a glimpse of a dark shadow disappearing over the mountain crest.

This was not the position he wanted to be in. There were two likely possibilities. She would fire at him again, from above, as soon as he was within range, or lie in wait for him when he reached the summit. He'd be an easy target, climbing up the rock face and either way he would be just as dead. .

The snow was heavier now and Vidarh blinked the flakes from his eyes, at the same time giving thanks again that he was so familiar with the terrain. He closed his eyes and visualised the level ground at the top of the ridge. By teleporting again so soon, he was depleting his energy resources, but he had little choice.

He used all his concentration to remember this particular area of the mountain. There was no room for error. If he got it wrong, he'd be saving Hedrohan the trouble of killing him.

His calculations and memory did not fail him. He felt a momentary satisfaction as he saw, in the half-light, the fleeting look of astonishment that passed across the Salmaran woman's face when he appeared several metres in front of her. It was replaced by an expression of disdain as she raised her heavy weapon.

Vidarh darted beneath an outcrop of rock a second before she fired, and sent his own energy bolt whanging toward her as she sped toward a large boulder, firing again. The ground in front of him erupted in a shower of ice and shale. He rolled over to another rocky projection and fired once more.

The snow fell from the sullen sky in a curtain of flakes that made it even more difficult to see his opponent. A shadow crossed the periphery of his vision and he aimed his weapon, ducking down behind his rock to avoid the Salmaran's return fire. He sensed she was trying to get behind him, his advanced powers of perception alerting him to her intentions.

Vidarh turned and fired once more, trying to see through the veil of snow, which now obscured his vision. He knew she was injured, but could not discern how badly, although he was aware of an aura of pain adding to the anger that emanated from her.

His own injury did not trouble him, the bio-regenerator had ensured its efficient and accelerated healing but he knew he was weakening. Apart from the blood he had lost earlier, each time he teleported it drained more of his strength. If he risked teleporting again, to avoid the Salmaran's blaster fire, he might render himself so weak as to be unable to defend himself against her.

For the first time Vidarh acknowledged the possibility that he might not survive this fight...might never see his family, or Tamarith, again.

He clenched his jaw and shook the snowflakes out of his eyes. Whatever the cost, he had to defeat Hedrohan. If he did not and she was able to return to her ship, she might return with reinforcements. She had already devastated Niflheim with the disease inflicted on its inhabitants. He could not bear to contemplate what Tamarith might have been forced to endure as her captive, or what might have happened if they had been too late to rescue her. If he failed, she, and who knew how many of his countrymen, could be taken again, forced into slavery on a strange planet.

Where was Hedrohan now? Had his fire finally reached its target? A sharp wind blew the snow around in swirling eddies and the light was almost gone. At least the flakes looked smaller and were not falling as heavily as before. A flash of purple shimmered to his right. He fired and ducked back behind the rock. Almost immediately, his fire was returned.

This could go on all night, or at least until the power source of either of their weapons was exhausted, and it would be completely dark in minutes. He needed to draw her out into the open, to finish this. If Hedrohan could throw stones, so could he.

Vidarh looked at the boulder in front of him and lifted it with his mind. He released it, causing it to drop with a shuddering crash just behind where the Salmaran woman had taken shelter. It had the desired effect and she broke cover, bent low and running toward him, with the occasional backward glance, firing wildly.

He seemed to have succeeded in confusing her. She appeared to be unsure whether she was fighting one or two opponents. Concentrating on an outcrop of rocks to the right of Hedrohan, he aimed his weapon at her again, and teleported. At the same moment, Hedrohan threw herself to the ground and fired directly at where he had been a few seconds before. She let out a vicious curse. Where he had been there was now an empty expanse of snow. She was crouching, weapon ready, gazing around, searching for him with something obviously approaching bewilderment.

Vidarh smiled inwardly, from his cover behind the rocks. Apparently, the Salmarans were not yet fully familiar with the accomplishments of Niflheim's inhabitants. He shook his head, trying to rid himself of the dizziness that swept over him. He must not lose consciousness now, but was aware that by teleporting again he had rendered himself even weaker.

He raised his head above the rocks as he steadied his blaster and fired again. This time there was a strangled scream and Hedrohan fell to her knees before crumpling to the ground. He waited a few moments then peered over the rock, straining his eyes in the semi-darkness to see through the swirls of gusting snow. Hedrohan lay unmoving.

After a while, he inched his way toward her, with the utmost caution. Logic told him she should be dead. She had been too close to him to have survived the force of the energy weapon. Yet as he drew close to her motionless form, his mind warned him of danger and he felt an evil malevolence reaching out to him. It was too late to teleport. With the last of his remaining strength, he thrust himself backward, as far away as he could. At the same time, he used all the power of his mind to push her bulk away from him telekinetically, as the blast ripped into his side. The last thing he remembered, as blackness engulfed him, was his finger on the trigger button of his blaster, firing automatically, until he lost consciousness.

Vidarh had no idea how long he lay there, but when he opened his eyes again, night had fallen. For a minute or two, he was not sure whether the blackness was real or in his mind. It took him a while to remember recent events and to realize he was still on the frozen ground and there was nothing but silence. The pain that seared through him was worse than anything he had ever suffered before. His skin felt clammy and he shivered with cold, despite his heavy icecat wool coat.

He concentrated his mind on trying to contact Tamarith but realized he was too weak. He could no longer project his thoughts. He could neither 'hear' nor transmit messages. A cold wetness stung his eyes, and it wasn't from the thin flurry of snow that swirled around him, or the burning agony in his side.

His tears were for Tamarith, and the realisation he would never see her again.

****

Tamarith looked up at the mountain. How long had she been travelling? A dark, heavy silence lay over these peaks. Not the peaceful tranquillity of the mountains around Gladsheim, but a deadly hush, as if they kept a dreadful secret, unknown to any, save those who perished in their cold embrace. Flashes of her dreams came back to her, and she banished them to the far corners of her mind.

She lowered her head against the wind as she climbed the narrow track. She reached out to grasp any overhanging rock or wiry shrub she could reach, all the while sending messages to Vidarh, willing him to hear her, to respond.

There was nothing. Even the wind was silent, although it whipped her hair around her face and tugged at her long coat. She dared not hurry, although every nerve in her body urged her to. If she tripped and fell in the darkness on these mountains it might be hours before anyone found her, and she would be no use to Vidarh.

The higher she climbed, the more concerned she became. Why did he not answer? Had he really just closed his mind against any contact, or was there another reason she could not reach him? She shook her head to dispel the thought. They had linked minds, there was a bond between them now and she would surely know if he no longer lived.

Mercifully, the snow had ceased and the moon

showed a faint glimmer of light. Because of its present position in the sky relative to the red giant, it had an eerie, pinkish tinge, which seemed almost sinister, although she told herself she was being foolish.

She risked increasing the power on her wrist flare. The path had disappeared some time ago and the route up the side of the mountain was steep and littered with boulders of various sizes. There must have been a landslip here recently. Surely if Hedrohan were nearby, Tamarith would have heard sounds of shooting. Vidarh could not have been far behind the slaver. But what if she had defeated him?

Tamarith shivered and bit her lip. Then Hedrohan would kill her, too. It was unlikely she would survive another encounter with the Salmaran. She concentrated on climbing, searching for hand and footholds and straining her ears for any sound that might indicate Hedrohan or Vidarh were close. All the time she sent out messages to him, but if they reached him, he did not answer.

She kept climbing, losing all track of time. She stopped to rest. She'd had little sleep and not bothered to eat before she left the camp, and hunger and exhaustion took their toll. All at once she sniffed the air. Clouds of bitter-smelling smoke drifted in a haze above her. She turned her head to one side and concentrated on climbing as swiftly as she could without losing her footing.

It was almost a shock when at last she reached the rim. She eased herself onto the icy ground, and sat for a few moments to catch her breath. Smoke hung in the air and it was obvious there had recently been a fight with power weapons.

Vidarh! Vidarh, are you here?

No answer. Nothing but silence. Abandoning caution, she adjusted her flare to full beam and swung around, stretching her arm and illuminating the ground before her. Suddenly she stood rigid. Over to her right, a large black mound, obviously the Salmaran, or what was left of her, lay inert and lifeless, face downward.

She looked all around, flashing the light on her wrist, straining her eyes for some sign of Vidarh, while calling to him in her mind. She walked away from the Salmaran woman's body, and at last spotted Vidarh lying a considerable distance away.

His arms were flung out away from his sides, his fingers clenched around the butt of his blaster, his garments half covered in snow. She could detect no life-signs.

She ran toward him. Tears spilled down her cheeks and it seemed as if her heart would break.

Chapter Twenty-Two

Vidarh struggled through black, clinging mud, toward the light. Crawling ever upward, with interminable slowness, for what seemed an eternity. The darkness became a grey haze and little by little slackened its grip as he reached out to the brightness. When he opened his eyes at last, he saw, as if through a mist, the face that had invaded his dreams, her long, dark hair sweeping over her shoulders as she bent toward him. There *was* an afterlife, then...

But what was Tamarith doing there?

Her face came more sharply into focus and the surroundings seemed familiar. Perhaps he was not dead after all.

"Thank goodness, you're awake at last. Are you thirsty?"

He nodded and she held a cup to his lips.

"Careful, don't drink too fast, just sip."

"Where...where are we?"

She frowned, but only said, "We're in Sleipnir. You're in your family's home. Some of the people we rescued from the Salmarans' overland vehicle were from Sleipnir and directed us to your father's homestead.

He looked around and realized he was indeed home again. And Tamarith was with him. Was this good or bad? He noticed the dark shadows under her eyes, but her expression was impassive. He reached out to her with his thoughts, and was relieved to find he could now make a connection, although it took all his concentration. He had been afraid the loss of his telepathic powers might be permanent.

Tamarith. How...how did you find me?

How do you feel? Are you in any pain?

No. I'm fine. This was not altogether true, he actually felt very stiff and sore, but he was not going to worry Tamarith by telling her this. He was grateful to have awoken and found himself still alive. *How long has it been?*

You've been unconscious for three days. We were afraid we'd lose you, even though Dahll and Jess used the bio-regenerators to heal your wounds. You were suffering from loss of blood and exposure after lying out in the snow on the mountain for so long. Dahll and Jess brought you here in their hopper vehicle.

What about my father...my family. Has...has the sickness reached Sleipnir?

Hush, Vidarh, we'll talk later. You need to rest and get your strength back. I must tell Jess you're awake.

She half turned to leave, but he caught hold of her sleeve.

Please...I must know, tell me the truth—

She turned back and her expression told him, before her reply reached his mind. *I'm sorry, Vidarh. The virus has affected everyone here. Your parents and the rest of your family are very sick. I wish I could give you better news. Jess and Dahll are doing everything they can.*

Vidarh groaned, trying to keep his mind blocked, but could not hide his distress from her. *Is there...is there any hope for them?*

I think you should speak to Jess in a little while, when you have rested some more. They're caring for your family, and the others in the Sleipnir area.

How is Gullin?

It was a close thing, but he's recovering. Jess has spent a lot of time with him. She is a finer nurse than she will admit. It seems she had some training on Phidia and it's stayed with her.

She pulled the covers more closely around him. *Now you must rest.*

Vidarh tried to protest but his eyes felt heavy and he wondered if Tamarith had put a sleeping draught in the water he had just drunk. Minutes later, he was asleep again and once more his dreams were all of her.

****

When he opened his eyes again, Jess was sitting beside him. The drapes in the room were open and he looked out over the rolling pastures of Sleipnir. The land sparkled with a light frosting of snow, tinged pink with the late rays of the afternoon suns.

"How are you feeling now? Are you hungry? It's been a long time since you ate."

He was relieved to find the stiffness had left him and he had hardly any pain or soreness. "A lot better now, thanks. And yes. I am hungry."

"I'll be back in a moment."

When she returned, Jess carried a steaming bowl of broth and some hunks of crusty bread and slices of fresh fruit on a tray, which she set down on a small table. Then she helped Vidarh sit up and plumped some pillows behind his shoulders.

"Enjoy your meal. Is there anything else you would like?"

"No, this is fine, thanks. How are *you*...are you over the upset stomach you had when I nearly poisoned you?"

Jess grinned and nodded, although her cheeks flushed a little as she replied. "I'm fine, Vidarh, really. You should concentrate on getting well, yourself, not worry about me. Tamarith will be back to see you in a few hours. I've persuaded her to get some rest."

Vidarh raised an enquiring eyebrow.

"She needs to catch up on her sleep. She hasn't moved from your bedside for three days."

Vidarh allowed himself a moment to wonder if it was just kindness that had prompted Tamarith's care of him. Was he being foolish in hoping for something more?

"How did you find me?" he asked. "I was so weak I couldn't telepath. How did you know where I was?"

Jess gave him a knowing smile. "That was Tamarith. We'd pitched a shelter for the night but she insisted on going back to look for you. She followed you up the mountain and contacted Melind when she found you, barely alive. She wouldn't leave you."

She paused. "I don't know how she did it, but somehow she kept you warm and alive, using some sort of kinetic energy. At first light, Dahll went back for the hopper. Tamarith kept in touch telepathically to guide Dahll to where you were. Luckily, the snow had stopped, or he wouldn't have been able to see to fly it, but he found you both on the mountain and brought you back."

Vidarh stopped, the spoon halfway to his lips. "What about Hedrohan?"

"They found her body and left it for the scavengers." Jess's eyes darkened for a moment. "Another storm was threatening. Getting you back safely was their priority. We used the regenerator on your wounds but you didn't regain consciousness until yesterday."

Vidarh drew in his breath in relief, thankful to have the slaver's death confirmed. "What about the Salmaran who was left on board the overlander? The prisoners put him to sleep for a while, but he wouldn't have been unconscious for more than a few hours."

"We think he must have taken the overlander and hidden in the mountains. Dahll went back to where we left it, but it had disappeared." Jess's expression grew serious. "He'd hoped to seize it and use it instead of the hopper. Our vehicle only holds four people at the most, and he had to make several trips."

"Is there any news of the other prisoners, the ones Hedrohan had already taken back to the ferry?"

"Yes, they're all safe. Dahll took a small party in the hopper and found the ferry in the barren lands of Muspell. They managed to get the prisoners off and bring them back here."

After a moment, Vidarh smiled a little self-consciously. "They all owe their lives to you and Dahll...as do I."

"And to Tamarith," she reminded him. "She kept you alive, and if it wasn't for her we'd never have found you. Even so, we only just reached you in time." She shook her head slowly with an expression of amazement on her face. "I don't know how you dodged Hedrohan's fire. You must've been lucky, normally a blaster at close range would have ripped you to pieces. As it was, it tore a chunk out of your side, and if Tamarith hadn't found you when she did, you'd have bled to death." She paused by the door, "I think that's enough questions for now. You need to rest. Don't forget to call if you need anything."

****

Again Vidarh slept. He did not wake again until late next morning. When there was a knock on his door, and it opened, for all the esteem in which he held Jess, he was pleased to see Tamarith standing there with a tray.

Good morning, I've brought you some breakfast.

He eased himself up in the bed and gave what he realized was a rather sheepish grin. *Thanks. I feel guilty about being waited on. I'll get up soon. I want to see my father and brothers.*

Your fever's gone, and you look much better than

184

you did. You'd better check with Jess, though. You've been pretty sick. Actually, it was 'touch and go' whether you'd make it.

I understand it was largely due to you that I did. Jess said you stayed with me for three days.

She looked away for a moment. *Someone had to watch you, and Jess was busy tending to Gullin. Between her and Dahll they saved both your lives. We have so much to be grateful to them for.*

She turned to leave the room, but Vidarh called her back.

Tamarith, please, sit with me for a while, if you can spare the time, that is.

Of course. She turned in the doorway and came back into the room. She drew up a chair, not too close to the bed, and seated herself.

Vidarh gulped down large mouthfuls of food, casting sideward glances at Tamarith as she looked through the window. Her hair shimmered in the sunlight and her sweet curves caused a flame of longing to set his blood on fire. Was there any chance she might feel the same way? He fumbled in his mind, trying to find the words to tell her how he felt, longing to tell her but afraid of her reaction.

She took the tray when he finished. *Was there something you wanted to talk to me about?*

Now was his chance. He did not normally find it difficult to put his feelings across, but all at once his confidence left him.

I just wanted to thank you....for...for what you did. Jess told me you guided Dahll to where I was. You saved my life.

Well, I couldn't have done it without Dahll's help. He and Jess—

How did you know where to find me? And that I was still alive?

She hesitated for a moment. *I...I just knew. As Gullin knew I was still alive when Hedrohan first*

185

captured me.

Vidarh studied her closely. Siblings were invariably aware of death or danger affecting one of them, and Tamarith was more than usually gifted. She'd probably been able to sense where he was in the same way, because of her heightened ability. Was that all it was? Or was there a new closeness between them since their minds had touched, that had told her he still lived, and led her to him? He longed to reach out with his thoughts, to let her feel the emotions that filled his heart, and ask the questions in his mind.

She stood with the tray in her hands, her eyes lowered. *If I saved your life, you also saved mine. You know I was ready to die when I fell into the chasm.*

Vidarh nodded, wanting to take her in his arms, to hold her close and tell her she had more to live for than she realized. Then the moment was gone and she headed for the door.

He cursed himself for behaving like some lovesick youth, too shy to tell the woman he loved how he felt. Until now, there had not been much room in his life for romance. The girls in the village near his family's homestead were pleasant enough, but none of them had made him feel the way Tamarith did. None had ever robbed him of his self-assurance like this, or filled him with desire merely by being near him.

He banished the thought from his mind as he reminded himself his father and brothers were critically ill and might not recover. He should be thinking of them now.

He washed and dressed, then made his way down the stairs to the main living area, where he was pleased to find Gullin, looking pale but otherwise his usual self, seated beside Jess. At least he could see his family and learn how widespread the sickness was.

****

"So everyone in Sleipnir has the sickness?"

Jess nodded grimly. "I'm afraid so."

The light faded, the glow of the setting suns reflecting off the snow. They had been to check on Vidarh's father and brothers. Vidarh was resting again, this time in the main living area, but in a sombre mood. His family, like most of the inhabitants of Sleipnir, it seemed, were barely conscious and showing no signs of improvement.

"We've managed to stabilise their condition," Jess told him, "but there's nothing more we can do." She sighed, looking very serious. "If only we could have reached them in time to administer the vaccine." She paused. "Dahll and I have been discussing the situation. We're going back to the *Quest* to try to ascertain if the shield has been lifted. We need to get to Phidia. It's our only hope for a cure."

Vidarh reached out and touched her arm. "We owe so much to you and Dahll already. We'll never be able to repay you."

"I only hope we'll be able to get through, and find the cure in time," Jess said, with a quick smile. "And as for repayment, the debt is mine. It's the least I can do for the kindness Tamarith and your people showed me when I last visited Gladsheim."

"Before you leave, can you show me what's needed—I want to know how to tend my family while they're sick."

Before Jess could reply, Tamarith appeared.

"It's good to see you up and about again," she said, nodding in Vidarh's direction and seating herself by the window.

"It seems I'm the only one from Sleipnir who isn't sick. I never thought I'd be grateful for nearly being killed."

187

"At least we know the vaccine the *Quest's* computer came up with works," Jess said. Everyone who used it is unaffected."

"How are the people at Gladsheim faring?" Vidarh asked Tamarith. "Are Thamri and Freya all right, and Rhenn and the others?"

Tamarith nodded. "They're fine. Both Gullin and I have been in contact with Thamri. She's been terribly worried, because of course she immediately knew something had happened to Gullin, and although Melind and I tried to reassure her, until Gullin was strong enough to contact her himself, she feared the worst."

While they had been talking, Vidarh had not been able to shake off a sense of anticipation—-or was it foreboding? A feeling something was approaching, something powerful and immense. He noticed Tamarith's frequent glances out of the window, as if expecting something or someone. Her mind remained closed and he was loathe to try to fathom what she was thinking. He was even more wary of intruding, now, after the incident in Loki's Chasm, but he could not help wondering if she sensed the same thing he did.

"Were all the Salmarans killed?" he wondered aloud.

Jess nodded. "Yes, all except the one who got away in the overlander." Vidarh hesitated, wondering whether to voice his suspicions. Could the Salmaran who escaped have managed to get a message to the mother ship? Were they now returning? Was it their presence he felt? Had they been able to pass through the barrier that had prevented the *Quest* from leaving?

But no, this feeling he had, this sense of something drawing close, was more powerful than anything that had emanated from the Salmarans, and somehow not as menacing.

"What about the people we rescued from the Salmaran overlander," he asked, in an attempt to take his mind off what he decided must be a trick of his imagination.

"We lost three of them in the fight with the Salmarans when Gullin was injured," Tamarith said soberly. "They were hit by blaster fire at point blank range. Several of the others were badly hurt but Dahll healed them with the regenerator. They've all returned to their homes now."

"Is Melind all right?" he asked, "I haven't seen her since—"

"Yes, she's outside with Dahll, somewhere," Jess told him. Vidarh glanced again at Tamarith. She was still staring fixedly out of the window. The sense of something powerful approaching was even stronger now. Before he could ask Tamarith whether she was feeling the same thing, there was a roar, like approaching thunder, but deeper, and continuous. All at once the twilight from outside winked out as if extinguished by an invisible hand, replaced by a soft, incandescent light.

All three came to their feet, just as Dahll and Melind burst through the door. Something like a shockwave hit Vidarh, as Melind's thoughts reached him, unchecked.

Come quickly, you must see. I think Niflheim is being invaded.

Chapter Twenty-Three

Jess was already halfway through the door, her hand grasping Dahll's arm, with Tamarith at her heels. Vidarh followed close behind. Once outside, all four looked at the sky. Vidarh gasped. The *Quest* had been awe-inspiring enough to a people unused to spacecraft landing on their planet, but this was something else!

The ship's bulk filled the sky, as far as he could see, and cast its illumination over the snow-clad landscape. The light came not only from the viewports all along the hull but reflected from the body of the ship itself.

After a momentary feeling of panic, Vidarh's mind filled with a great sensation of peace. He relaxed, convinced that whatever the craft was, it did not mean them any harm. He glanced at Tamarith, standing next to him, and knew she felt it, too.

The others, including Jess and Dahll, also appeared to have any feelings of apprehension dispelled. They gazed in fascination at the behemoth dominating the heavens above them.

As he watched, a hazy, many-colored mist formed, coalescing into a huge, vaguely humanoid shape. Other similar figures stood in the background, shimmering and indistinct, but he could not be sure of their number.

Greetings. Do not be fearful.

The voice was telepathic. Vidarh cast a swift look at his companions, and realized everyone, including Dahll and Jess, also heard it.

We have been watching this, our home planet, since the time it was first colonised by your people. We do not wish to harm you. It is not our nature to kill or destroy, and we are saddened by the events of recent weeks.

Who are you? Vidarh asked. *This is your home world?*

That is so. We are the Etzlolendl. In the far distant past, while life was still evolving on the planet you call 'Earth', this world was green and lush. Even the poles were warm and habitable, although our people preferred the tropical areas that covered most of the planet. Large areas were, of course, desert-land, but even these we were able to irrigate and utilise. The energy we received from our double star was sufficient for our needs and far greater than now.

The alien ambassador paused in its narrative and Vidarh looked at his companions. The rapt attention apparent on their faces told him they had all received the same message.

Why did you leave? he asked.

As knowledge increased and our technology became ever greater, our scientists realized that in less than a million years one of the two suns would become a red giant and consume our world. The most advanced scientists came together and fashioned a plan. We would move a gigantic asteroid from its course so that it passed nearer the planet.

"Forgive me for asking," Dahll said, "but that must have been an immense undertaking, even for a highly technologically advanced civilisation. Accepting that you were able to accomplish it, how did that prevent the death of this world?"

We will explain. Using robotic spacecraft we attached small rockets to the asteroid to manoeuvre its course. This enabled us to exploit some of the space rock's orbital energy and use it to move this

191

world into an orbit slightly farther away from the sun that we knew would become a red giant.

The entity paused, as if to give them chance to assimilate this information.

We then sent the asteroid back on a course around a giant planet on the edge of our system to regain some of its orbital energy by stealing it from the giant. We made the rock continue on a long, elliptical orbit. By keeping a robot crew permanently in stationary orbit around that planet and bringing the asteroid back every few thousand years, we were able to edge our home planet, which you now call 'Niflheim', to a safe distance from the red giant. The figure paused again, as if inviting a reply.

Surely, Gullin put in, *that must have meant a great reduction in the temperature of this world. How could you adapt to the tremendous climate changes?*

Initially, by building very large, orbiting solar reflectors, aimed toward our planet. This prevented it from cooling down too rapidly. We realized, of course, that the conditions here would eventually be too cold for our species, although not so severe as to be unable to support life at all. The small G-type sun was at an optimum distance for its energy to be sufficient to support certain life forms, like those who now inhabit it. Those of us who were left after the last 'pass' of the asteroid, departed from our old world forever. We made our home on a new planet in a star system our scientists had discovered thousands of years before and which we began to colonise soon after the plan was first formed.

We kept a close watch on our home world, and were not surprised when the people of Earth settled on it. Some of the cooler areas of Earth were not dissimilar to the more temperate areas here. We noted with satisfaction that only the strongest of mind and the most determined stayed and built communities, while the others returned to Earth.

There was another pause, before the being continued with, *It amused us that you chose to name this planet after the mythical land of the gods of an ancient Terran civilisation. Discerning the settlers were peacefully inclined, we hid our presence and watched your population grow and spread across the habitable areas. We observed how you developed telepathy and learnt to communicate across the continents and even into the vast reaches of space itself. It pleased us that you employed the natural resources of the planet, turning your backs on Earth's destructive resource-depleting technology.*

Melind stepped forward. *So we are living on your planet—your world. Have you....have you come to claim it back?* It seemed a naïve question, but one that had also crossed Vidarh's mind.

The response emanating from the life form sounded suspiciously like laughter. *No, this world has become far too cold for our species. Although we do have the technology to move it closer to the G-type or even to a new solar system altogether, we have outgrown this planet. Besides, nothing in the Universe is the property of any race or being. We are merely its protectors and keepers. We are happy that you have settled here. We have monitored your progress and seen that you are a peaceable people. When we discerned another race had brought sickness and violence we knew we had to intervene, although normally we would not interfere in the affairs of other civilizations.*

Vidarh glanced toward Dahll and saw him exchange a meaningful look with Jess.

"Then it was you," she said. "You put the forcefield around Niflheim—to stop the Salmarans landing any more slavers. We thought the Salmarans had somehow managed to develop it and used it to stop us leaving to try and find a cure for the sickness."

The race you call Salmarans is a savage one and will never evolve to the degree that could produce anything as complex as the band of energy we have placed around this planet. We regret it prevented your leaving, but had we made a breach in the ring, the Salmaran mother ship would also have been able to slip through and would, in all probability, have destroyed your ship as well as enslaving the settlers. If they had succeeded, they would have brought more ships. We could not allow such a cruel and barbaric lifeform to take over our home world.

Vidarh swallowed. *Are you willing to allow us to continue living here?*

We have no reason to want you to leave. Where would you go—back to an overcrowded, polluted and climatically unstable Earth? No. Niflheim—there was a slight pause after the Terran name, although it was pronounced with perfect accuracy—*is of no further use to us. You are welcome to stay as guardians of our home world. The entity paused again. Do you have any more questions for us before we leave?*

"Please," Jess said, "now that the Salmarans are defeated, can you let us through the barrier? We need to fetch help to cure the sickness the Salmarans inflicted on the settlers—"

To allow the barrier to remain open would be to leave this planet in danger. We will give you a key. Programming it into your ship's navigation system will enable you to pass through safely and the rift will close behind you. When you wish to return, the barrier will recognise your ship and reopen. Perhaps, at some future time, you will learn to defend yourselves, without resorting to the violence inherent in the nature of humanoid species. Until then it will protect this world from those who would be your enemies.

I would like to ask a question, if I may, Tamarith

addressed the Etzlolendl for the first time. *There are several ancient statues in the caves of the mountains that cross between the two Great Plains. Did your people carve them—and is that what you look like?*

The answer to your first question is yes. We fashioned the statues in the hope that if another species colonised this world, they would relate to the statues. They would know another species, more ancient than they could possibly comprehend, had inhabited this planet before them. The answer to your second question is no, that is not our physical appearance. We shaped the figures into a humanoid form, since most of the higher intelligences on what you term 'M' type planets are similar in appearance, albeit with slight differences.

But why would you do that? Vidarh asked, unable to hide his curiosity. *Why not make the statues represent how you look?*

There was a long pause and Vidarh wondered if he had overstepped the boundaries.

Then the entity 'spoke' again.

We thought it wise not to. We have noted that humans, however well intentioned, either fear or seek to destroy what they do not understand. You could never destroy us and we do not wish you to fear us. Now we will leave. We charge you with the care of this world as once we cared for it. Prosper and live in peace.

As Vidarh watched, the mist swirled, the colours changing and brightening with what looked like lightning flashes. It turned gold, forming an upward swirling spiral. In a moment it dissipated and blended into the radiance cast by the ship itself. He heard Jess give a soft cry and saw her step back, as if hit by an unseen force. A mighty wind suddenly bent the skeletal forms of the trees until it seemed they might snap, sending the group scurrying back indoors.

195

They peered through the large window as the glowing ship rose vertically, with a roar that was almost more than their ears could stand. Within seconds, it had disappeared from sight above the layer of clouds.

For a moment, they stood in silence, too stunned to think, let alone speak.

"So those are the true inhabitants of Niflheim," Gullin said at last. "Did everyone hear them...him?" he paused and Vidarh realized the telepathic 'voice', if that is what it could be called, had been neither male nor female, and it was not even possible to be sure whether it had been of a single being, or many. Gullin glanced at Dahll and Jess, his question obviously directed at them.

Jess nodded, looking at Dahll. "Yes, we both 'heard' it too. At least we know the Salmarans didn't form the barrier and that we can get through it now."

Dahll put his hand on her arm. "Something happened to you out there. You looked like you had some sort of power shock. Are you all right?"

"Something very powerful touched me. I wasn't prepared for it, that's all." Slowly she opened her fingers. In her palm lay a tiny, shining disc.

"An encryption chip?"

"The key. If we can figure a way of getting this hooked into the *Quest's* navigation computer, it'll open up the barrier, and we can try to fetch help from the Phidians before it's too late."

Vidarh looked at her, hardly daring to hope there was a chance of saving his family. He had to face facts. He knew his brothers and parents were critically ill, and even though their condition had been stabilised, it would take something like a miracle for them to recover.

"Try not to worry," Jess said. "We'll do all we can to get help in time. I think we should leave as soon as is practical. If the Phidians can find a cure we may be in time to save your family."

"The hopper should be fully charged again by now," Dahll said. He looked across at Gullin, Melind and Tamarith.

"We'd offer you a lift to Gladsheim, but unfortunately the vehicle won't take us all."

"Thank you for thinking of it," Gullin said, "but Vidarh has offered to lend us some ponies for our return. Thamri says ours arrived home a few days ago—including Flyer," he added with a smile at Melind. "Naturally I am anxious to get back to Thamri and the baby, but she insists I stay here a few days longer, to fully recover." He looked at Dahll. "When will you leave?"

"At first light tomorrow. I'd rather not fly the hopper at night because of the mist. I hope when we next meet, we'll have the cure for the virus and you'll be able to forget the Salmarans were ever here."

****

True to their word, Jess and Dahll left at dawn the following day. The return to Gladsheim did not take as long as Jess had feared. With the onset of summer, the weather had changed for the better. Although a thick mist still covered the land in the early morning, by mid-day it had dissipated enough to allow the solar panels on the hopper to absorb sufficient sunlight to stay energised for the whole journey.

They had an enthusiastic, if slightly tearful reunion with Thamri. To their relief neither she nor Freya showed any symptoms of the sickness. As soon as they could, they left the settlement and boarded the *Quest*. Any delay could be fatal to Vidarh's family and the other Nifls affected by the Salmaran virus.

The computer had produced several thousand

more vials of the serum. Hermot accompanied them to the *Quest* and took as many back to Gladsheim as he could. Even if the Phidians found a cure, it was sensible to have stocks of the vaccine in case the sickness should ever re-occur. According to the computer analysis, though, that was unlikely, especially as the vaccine had proved so effective.

Soon after lift-off, Dahll fed the data from the 'key' the Etzlolendls had given them into the computer's decoder.

While he concentrated on formatting and programming the results, Jess made good her promise to Vidarh and presented herself to the ship's medical computer.

She was elated when the results proved to be exactly what she expected. She never really believed she had succumbed to the virus, but it made sense to check her physical condition to be sure. As she went through the detailed information the system provided, she chuckled inwardly...well, she had never been one to do things by halves.

After checking and recording the computer records, most of which was technical and confirmed what they already knew about the pathogen, she returned to the Flight Deck.

Dahll looked up from the main console. "Hello, sweet. What have you been up to?"

"Oh, just checking the data on the virus. Nothing new, but it might help the Phidians. Have you finished programming the key into the nav-system yet? Will it work?"

"We'll soon find out," Dahll said. Before he could activate the relevant control, the main computer's vocal system cut in.

Attention. Unidentified vessel ahead. Hull sensors register we have been scanned. Reciprocal scanning in progress.

"Oh no, not now!" Jess glanced at the forward

observation screen and the pulsating blip that suddenly appeared. She read off the data and for a moment, she and Dahll stared at each other in alarm.

"Full visual image on observation screen, Seattle," she commanded. She drew in her breath. "Dahll, is that what I think it is?"

"I'm afraid so," Dahll said grimly. "It's a Salmaran ferry. She's dead ahead of us, and turning. According to our sensors, she's about to open fire."

Chapter Twenty-Four

"Seattle! Shield!" Jess flung herself at the controls as Dahll took over the weapons array.

"Fire plasma bolt," he hissed at the computer. The ship rocked at the shield's deflection of the first salvo. Jess used all her piloting skills to dodge the next onslaught. The Salmaran ferry was large and bristling with weaponry. For a fleeting moment, Jess wondered why a transit vehicle should be so well armed. However, from her knowledge of the aggressive race of slavers, she decided they'd probably arm any vehicle if there was a chance they'd meet a potential prey who might fight back.

"It's nothing less than a small fighting ship," Dahll said between gritted teeth. "It's armed like a warship. If that's the ferry, I hate to think what the main slave ship's like."

Before Jess could reply, a clutch of plasma bolts required her attention. Deftly she applied the *Quest's* side thrusters. Immediately the Salmaran ship changed course and the *Quest* shuddered as another volley hit the shield.

"I'm not sure how much more of this the *Quest* can take at this close range," she gasped. "I just hope the shield holds."

"It'll hold," Dahll assured her as he ordered a well-aimed shot at the enemy ship's bows. "It's a drain on the power reserves though. We're twenty one per cent down on bank three already."

Jess manoeuvred the *Quest on a* zigzag course, trying to avoid the Salmarans' fire, and at the same time keep the ship steady enough for Dahll to take aim. Human skill was still more accurate than the on-board computers, sophisticated though they were. Not for the first time, she was grateful for the instantaneous response of the *Quest.*

Despite her size and slowness, compared to their little hyper-speedster, the Salmaran vessel swooped and turned with surprising agility to avoid their fire, at the same time striving to fire a fatal salvo.

"Fire plasma bolt—now!" Dahll commanded the computer again, his voice gruff with concentration. Jess watched on the observation screen as another fiery sphere seared toward them. She banked the ship sharply to one side, as Dahll aimed yet another shot at the enemy.

The Salmaran vessel also altered direction, firing again, and Jess rammed the *Quest* upward. The ship trembled along the length of her hull as the aft shield took the full impact.

"That was a bit too close for comfort," she muttered, and immediately shielded her eyes with her hands, looking away from the scanner as a blinding flash blotted out everything else for a moment, before the screen returned to the darkness of empty space.

The enemy ship is destroyed, the computer intoned without expression. *Long-range scan detects no trace of other hostile vessels.*

Jess and Dahll looked at each other in relief. "Damage report?" Dahll asked, turning back to the control panel.

A small amount of superficial damage to the stern. Auto repair systems initialised.

"That *was* a near thing," Dahl admitted. "The Salmaran ferry must have stayed cloaked until the last possible moment. He must have monitored us since we left Niflheim."

"Yes." Jess tossed her hair back with a frown. "I knew we should have destroyed it when we rescued the prisoners, although I suppose it would have taken more than a few mines to do it. I wonder where the main slave ship is?"

"On its way back to Salmar with any luck," Dahll said, with feeling. "They're certainly not in this sector of space, or our scanners would have detected them. Just in case, though, we'd better get out of here. The sooner we go hyper so they can't track us, the better."

They seated themselves, activated the safety restraints, and Dahll, taking the main controls, gave the command to the navigation computer. The instruments on the control panel registered the forcefield ahead, although on-screen it looked like empty space.

As they approached, the computer sounded the alarm and prepared to shut down the drives. Dahll checked the control panel, glanced back at Jess, then keyed in a sequence of numbers. A wall of blue flame scintillated and then died. At once, the alarm ceased. Dahll eased the ship forward and accelerated. There was no resistance and the computer registered no obstacle to their progress. A few moments later, he checked their position.

"We're through—it worked!"

****

"So that's why we've come here to ask your help," Jess finished, sitting forward in her seat in the comfortable office of Yan-Kloor, the Senior Administrator of the Main Phidian Medical Centre. "Do you think you'll be able to find a cure for the people of Niflheim?" She tried not to look too anxious but her concern was difficult to hide.

Yan-Kloor smiled, his deep purple oval eyes twinkling against the silvery blue sheen of his skin, looking first to her and then to Dahll. "Our experts are already working on the sample, I'm sure it won't take them too long to find a formula to combat the pathogen."

"Thank you. Thank you so much," Jess said. "The inhabitants of Niflheim will be so grateful, without your help many more of their people will die."

Yan-Kloor rose to his feet. "I trust we will not be too late. We are glad to have the opportunity to help you. Those of us who are aware of the circumstances surrounding your near fatal injury in the battle with the invaders of this planet, know full well that Phidia would be under alien occupation now if it were not for you. We will always be in your debt."

"But you gave me back my life. There is no debt left to pay."

"And I, for one, have every reason to be grateful to you, for saving her," Dahll said.

"Then let us just say we are glad to be able to help out with a favour, and also add to our medical knowledge."

Wordlessly, Jess put her hand on Yan-Kloor's arm and placed a soft kiss on his cheek. She and Dahll bade the old physician a polite goodnight and settled themselves in the small but comfortable room that had been made ready for them.

"There's nothing more we can do now except wait for Yan-Kloor and his scientists to come up with a cure," Jess said, sinking onto the comfortable bed.

"Yes, best get some rest while we can—you've been looking a bit tired lately." Dahll sat down beside her and placed his arm around her, kissing her gently. "You sure you're all right?"

"I'm fine—in fact I'm more than fine."

She laid her head on his shoulder and closed her eyes, enjoying the peace of the moment. "We've come such a long way, you and I since we first met, here on Phidia."

"That's true." He pushed a stray lock of hair away from her eyes. "You were all I've ever wanted, from the moment I first saw you. Back then I never thought..."

He paused and drew her closer. "I am so thankful to have you for my Lady. I couldn't ask for anything more."

Jess turned to look at him then, knowing now was the time. Taking both his hands in hers, no longer able to conceal her excitement, she gazed up at him and grinned broadly.

"There's something I want to tell you. I didn't have chance while we were on our way here."

"Oh?" His smile turned curious. "What adventure do you have in store for us, next?"

She laughed with sheer joy, loving this man who was so willing to indulge her thirst for adventure. She planted a kiss on his furrowed brow, and knew she couldn't keep the sparkle or the love from her eyes as she said, "That depends. But whatever we do, I suggest we make the most of our time together for the next few months—because after that we're going to be a little busy. And it won't be just the two of us."

His eyes widened in disbelief. "Jess? You're telling me we're going to have a baby?" The look of stunned delight on his face confirmed that, despite his surprise, he was as thrilled at the prospect as she was.

"No, my love," she said, wrapping her arms around his neck. "We're having twins!"

****

Gullin kept his promise to Thamri, to rest for a few days. However, on the third day after Jess and Dahll had returned to the *Quest*, he announced he and his sisters would leave in the morning.

After the evening meal, Gullin bade Vidarh goodnight, saying he wanted to get a good night's sleep before the following day's journey. He suggested Melind do the same and suddenly Vidarh found himself alone with his thoughts.

He realised he had not seen Tamarith for some time, and, deciding she must be somewhere outside, put on his coat and went in search of her. He knew this might be the last chance he would have to tell her of his feelings. Tomorrow she would leave for Gladsheim and he might never see her again.

He found her with Malmooth, at the back of the house near the outbuildings, watching the sky. She gazed toward the mountains that brooded behind the homestead. The pearly pink rays of the moon filtered through the mist, which hung from the trees, illuminating her slim silhouette and giving her an almost ethereal appearance.

I wondered where you were. Gullin and Melind have already turned in.

She continued to look across at the mountains, and his heart ached as he sensed her mind was closed even more tightly against him.

I know. I just wanted to say goodbye to Malmooth. There won't be a lot of time tomorrow. She turned, not quite looking at him, her hand on the animal's neck. *He's recovered well, but I don't think he's strong enough to walk all the way to Gladsheim. Will you look after him for me until he's ready to make his own way back?*

Of course, I'll be happy to.

They stood in silence for several minutes. *I...suppose I should turn in, too.* Tamarith's silvery tones in his mind sounded hesitant, a little strained even. *I don't expect we'll see each other again after tomorrow.*

Vidarh caught his breath and tried to look indifferent, although his heart leapt in his chest at the thought that perhaps, even now, there might be a shred of hope. She'd filled his mind, lately. He hardly seemed capable of concentrating on anything else, although he had done his best to hide his feelings from her, certain she cared nothing for him.

Now something in her manner, as well as her question, made him wonder if he was mistaken.

Would that matter to you? He stepped closer, willing her to open her mind to him, to let him see what was really in her heart.

She did not quite look at him as she replied: *I'll miss your company. I feel we've become...friends.*

I could always teach you to teleport yourself, and you could visit me. You're very gifted. It was your own power that got you out of Loki's Chasm. Teleportation will come easily to you with a little practice.

I think you could teach me a lot. If you hadn't reached out to me, I would never have been able to do it alone. She hesitated and lowered her eyes again, obviously struggling with something, and reluctant to reveal it.

Vidarh attempted to dispel the awkwardness between them. *I don't think you realize how gifted you are. I'm sure there are things you could teach me, as well. We could learn from each other.*

Tamarith dropped her guard, just a little, but enough for him to feel the loneliness and uncertainty in her. He reached down to pet Malmooth and tried to think of a way to tell Tamarith how he felt about her.

His fingers brushed against hers. The power that surged through him was like nothing he had ever experienced before. The last time they had touched hands was in Loki's Chasm, when they were both in deadly danger and their thoughts needed to be concentrated on one thing, teleporting themselves to safety.

This was different.

They looked at each other in shock.

She tried to draw away her hand, but he tightened his fingers around it, and raised it to his lips. He felt her tremble from head to toe, like a captured bird.

He looked at her in awe. This lovely woman had saved his life. She'd fearlessly fought a powerful alien, yet she trembled at his touch. He drew a deep breath and it took all his willpower to refrain from crushing her to him. He ached to kiss her, to quench the fire that coursed through his body. He pulled her toward him, and placing his hand beneath her face, gently lifted her chin, compelling her to look at him. His eyes locked on hers, and he forced himself to keep control, not to rush, not to frighten her away before he had chance to tell her what he needed her to know.

Tamarith, do you remember what I said to you in Loki's Chasm, when our minds met?

Yes, I...I remember. I was prepared to die and you called out to me. She hesitated, and seemed unsure of herself. *I thought you were trying to...to make me open my mind to you, so you could help me save myself—*

That much was right, but how could she believe he would profess his love if it were not true? Even now, she doubted him. By the Universal Spirit, it was difficult enough to control his body any time he was around her! How could she *not* know?

Tamarith, I meant it. Look into my mind and you will see. He cupped her face in both his hands, looking deep into her eyes and emptying his thoughts of everything except his love for her. Gradually he felt the barriers in her mind melt away as his thoughts reached out to hers. She closed her eyes, and when she opened them again, her long eyelashes were damp, her eyes bright with tears.

When you went after Hedrohan, and were nearly killed and I found you, so badly injured, your life force was so weak I couldn't feel it. I thought...I thought you were dead. I couldn't bear it and I realized then, that I...I love you, Vidarh.

Vidarh studied her face, wondering if his mind was deceiving him, making him imagine what he longed for her to say. With the tips of his fingers, he tenderly wiped away the tears that glistened on her cheeks. *Dahll?* he asked, at last. *You're no longer in love with him?*

She looked startled for a moment, then obviously realized Vidarh had sensed her thoughts of Dahll when they merged minds in the chasm. *No, he was never mine. We were not meant for each other. I always knew it, but I couldn't let go—until I met you.*

Despite the words she sent into his mind, part of her still remained guarded. He felt her vulnerability, her fear of laying her soul bare to him. She was protecting herself like a nervous, wounded animal, afraid to love again, afraid of being hurt.

I love you, Tamarith. I would never knowingly do anything to hurt you. Never. You mean everything to me. I would rather die than see you unhappy.

He felt her mind open completely to him, then, and the blinding surge of love that swept over him permeated every nerve in his body, told him more than words ever could. He took her in his arms and kissed her, holding her so close he could feel her heart pound against his chest. The warmth of her breasts against him, and the touch of her lips on his, sent something like an electrical current surging through him. White heat enveloped his body, liquid fire coursed through his veins.

She slipped her arms around him, still trembling, her mouth on his, yielding and passionate. None of Vidarh's previous experiences, such as they were, had ever felt like this. His mind had never linked so completely to another's.

Tamarith, I love you. I love you so much.

And I love you, Vidarh, more than I ever thought possible.

Chapter Twenty-Five

Tamarith leant against him, her heart pounding, her mind filled with so many emotions, so much love, that for a moment she felt she would lose her senses.

There's such a lot I want to know about you, so much I want to ask you, he murmured in her mind. She shivered as a sharp wind whistled through the trees and bit at her skin.

We can't stay out here. You're getting cold. With a swift movement Vidarh removed his coat and placed it around her shoulders. *Come with me—just for a little while.*

Clearly he was able to exercise amazing control over his own feelings and emotions. The passion...the longing that a moment ago had threatened to consume them both had faded, and she sensed a stillness fill Vidarh's mind. As she fought to control her own feelings the confusion faded, to be replaced by a feeling of calm and warmth—and an all-enveloping, protecting love.

The vision of a cosy, wooden cabin, sheltered in a hollow on the mountainside gradually formed in her mind, as it once more became as one with his. She felt an instant of freezing blackness, then suddenly they stood inside a building with solid walls. The moonlight streamed through the window and illuminated the single room enough to show the wide, comfortable couch against the wall, near the fireplace.

"That was—this is amazing!"

"And only the beginning of what we can share,"

Vidarh said with a smile.

His arms still around her, he glanced toward the hearth. The sticks and kindling, laid ready, immediately leapt into orange tongues of flame and soon the cabin was filled with a warm glow. Tamarith realized he had ignited the hearth with his mind. Yet another skill she had not known he possessed and one she also shared.

There is a lot we both have to learn about each other, she agreed.

Vidarh smiled that crooked smile of his, guided her to the couch and seated himself beside her. She sighed and laid her head on his shoulder, happier than she could ever remember being.

Where are we?

He kissed her temple gently. *We're in a small cabin belonging to my family, up in the hills. We use it for shelter if a blizzard brews up when we're tending the herd animals."*

Why did you bring me here?

I wanted to spend a little time with you, just the two of us—before you leave for Gladsheim tomorrow.

He loosed the simple ribbon holding back her hair, and she saw his smile widen in the moonlight as her locks escaped to cascade over her shoulders and spill over the edge of the couch.

I've never known a woman as lovely you. Vidarh's lips touched on her nose, then gently caressed her cheek, before returning to her mouth. The heat that flooded through her sent tingling thrills through her body. The pleasant musky scent of him made her senses swim.

Smoothing her hair with his hand, he kissed her again, long and soft. She closed her eyes and allowed her mind to float with his. It seemed their kiss would last forever, but at last they drew apart and sat with their arms around each other in the flickering firelight.

Warm in each other's embrace, they poured out their feelings, which until now they had kept hidden deep within the secret places of their minds.

Vidarh told her how from the moment her mind first touched his, he had felt drawn to her, without fully understanding why. When she asked, he also told her a little about his childhood, and how he had always felt out of place in the farming community he still lived in.

In return, she confessed how her feelings toward him had grown, almost without her realizing. How being able to contact him when she was imprisoned by Hedrohan had not only given her strength, but led to the acknowledgment that a special bond was being forged between them.

She snuggled even closer to him. *I didn't know I could ever feel so loved.*

And I didn't know I could grow to love anyone the way I do you.

Tamarith could not bear to think of being parted from him now. She gazed earnestly into his face. *Let me stay here in Sleipnir, with you...please. I don't want to go back to Gladsheim without you.*

He took both her hands in his, and pressed them to his lips. *No, it's best you return to your home. Our minds are forever linked now, so much that no distance can ever truly separate us. We will always be open to each other. I'm no farmer, Tamarith,* he went on, looking into her eyes, with an expression in his own that dispelled any last, lingering doubt. *That's something I've realized over the past few weeks. I promise, when Dahll and Jess return, and I know my family will recover and no longer need me, I will come to Gladsheim, and we'll never be apart again.*

His face in the light of the flickering flames, was grave as he went on, *should they not find a cure—or if it is too late and my parents and brothers don't make it—I will still come. I won't lose you now. I swear it.*

She nodded in mute acceptance and lifted her face to his.

He kissed her again, and they sat together in the firelight, neither wanting to break the enchantment that bound them.

The happiness that filled Tamarith's being was tinged with sadness that, for a while, this was all they would have. In a few hours she would leave for her family's home, and who knew when they would see each other again.

That's why I brought you here, Vidarh whispered in her mind. *To show you what it will be like—one day not too far distant. One day we'll sit in our own home, watching the flames flicker in the hearth, and we'll remember this moment.*

*He ran his fingers through her hair and kissed her again. For a long time they sat with their arms around each other, not even their thoughts disturbing the sanctity of the moment, until at last he s*tood and gently pulled her up with him, giving her one last, lingering kiss.

Best be getting back now, before we're missed.

He wrapped his arms around her and extinguished the fire with a glance. Reluctantly she forced herself to focus her mind with his for their return to the farmstead.

****

Hermot stepped from the room and glanced at the small group who had risen from their seats at his appearance.

"Well?" Vidarh asked, trying to prevent his voice giving away how apprehensive he felt. If it had not been for the presence of Dahll and Jess, he would have telepathed his question. Telepathy at its basic level made it easier to hide ones fears and anxieties.

"It's a little early to tell yet," the physician said,

"but they're responding well to the Phidian antiserum." He nodded to Dahll and Jess. "You have earned our gratitude. It looks like we'll be able to save the lives not just of Vidarh's family, but of the rest of the people who still survive. There's only one problem now—how are we going to get it to them?"

Silence reigned for a moment.

"The *Quest,*" Dahll said, almost casually, as if it were the natural solution.

The Nifls looked at him in amazement.

"But the *Quest* is a starship," Hermot said, staring at Dahll as if he had suddenly lost his senses.

"Don't worry about that," Dahll reassured him. "She's capable of flying in an atmosphere as well. We can travel to the other side of the continent in a fraction of the time it would take even with the hopper. I reckon we can get the serum to everyone on the planet who needs it in time to save them. We can land on the plains and use the hopper to reach the more inaccessible mountainous areas, and it's not as if Niflheim is densely populated."

An idea had been formulating in Vidarh's mind for some time now. He looked directly at Hermot. "I want to learn to be a healer, like you. I'm not cut out to be a farmer. My brothers and father will be quite capable of running the homestead without me, once they're fit again."

He glanced around the room, his lips set in determination. "I used to shy away from people. Now I realize I was being selfish in seeking my own company. I want to do something with my life—to help people. The last few weeks have shown me that even if we eradicate the sickness from Niflheim, there will always be accidents. People will always have need of surgeons and physicians, and I would like to train as one, myself."

Hermot nodded, then smiled. "It looks like I

have a new apprentice."

Vidarh smiled back. "It looks like you do."

"Good. The sooner you start, the better. If you can arrange for someone to care for your family while you're away, you can come with me and help with the vaccinations."

Vidarh was momentarily chagrined. The offer was one he would be foolish to refuse. But what about his family? He couldn't leave them, not until they were fully recovered.

"Much as Dahll and I hate being apart from each other," Jess said suddenly, "The *Quest's* really only built for two pilots. It might be a bit crowded with four on board. Why don't I stay here to look after your family while you three deliver the serum?"

"You would do that for me?"

Jess smiled. "Of course."

Vidarh nodded and smiled his thanks, another thing to be grateful to Jess Tarron for.

"Then it's settled," Hermot said. "We have all the homesteads in Sleipnir to visit first. Once we have vaccinated the folk here and covered the rest of Niflheim, if you're still set on being a healer, we can return to Gladsheim, and begin your training in earnest."

"Thank you," Vidarh said softly. "And I can promise you I'm not going to change my mind."

Chapter Twenty-Six

The evening was perfect. A warm breeze played through the trees, sighing over the valley, and the moon shone across the lake. The water shimmered with splashes of incandescent colour as reflections of the Rainbow Bridge, and the light from the sparkling lanterns suspended from the trees lining the mosaic paths, mingled on its rippled surface.

A small band of players strode among the guests at the wedding feast. The music of their unique stringed instruments, soft and lilting, added to the ambience, already aglow with romance and celebration. The dancing newlyweds held each other close, gazed into each other's eyes, and seemed oblivious to everything else going on around them.

Jess leant her head on Dahll's shoulder. She sighed in contentment. "I'm so happy for her. I couldn't have wished a better husband for Tamarith than Vidarh."

Dahll smiled, his eyes softening with affection. "Matchmaker," he teased.

"Well, they're so right for each other. And Tamarith deserves to be happy. As happy as I am," she added, squeezing his arm.

He kissed the top of her head. "Any idea who that is with Melind?"

Jess followed his gaze. "I'm not sure. I think he's the son of one of Vidarh's neighbours."

"Didn't take Melind long to get over Vidarh," Dahll grinned. "She's been flirting with her new brothers-in-law all evening."

"Well, she's very young and she was always less

serious than Tamarith. She still has a lot of growing up to do. I think she'll break a lot of hearts before it's her turn to settle down."

Jess smiled at Gullin as he and Thamri, holding Freya in her arms, walked toward them, dodging the throngs of jostling, laughing revellers.

"You must be very proud of Tamarith today, Gullin."

"I am, Jess. She does look beautiful. Vidarh will make her a fine husband. I am glad he intends to stay here when he's finished his training, rather than taking her back to Sleipnir." Gullin paused. "You and Dahll will always have our gratitude. Things could so easily have turned out differently. We could be mourning our loved ones, instead of celebrating a wedding."

"I'm just relieved the Phidians were able to find the cure," Jess said. "And thanks to the Etzlolendl no-one will be able to land on Niflheim again without the key to the barrier, so you should be safe from people like the Salmarans in the future."

Thamri handed Freya carefully to Gullin and slipped an arm around Jess, giving her an affectionate hug. "And it's not just a wedding we have to celebrate." She glanced across at Dahll. "I am so pleased for you both, and we are all very glad you were able to stay for Tamarith and Vidarh's special day."

Jess smiled and hugged her back, her gaze once more drawn to the young lovers in each other's arms, swaying in time to the music.

****

I wish this moment could last forever.

We will remember today always. I couldn't imagine a better way to start our life together than here, among all our friends and family.

Vidarh could not stop looking at his bride. Tonight Tamarith looked more beautiful than ever.

Her hair, free from restraint and gleaming in the light from the lanterns, cascaded like liquid obsidian to her ankles. Tiny silver-white flowers woven into the silky tresses looked, he thought whimsically, like miniature stars against the blackness.

Her ivory velvet robe sparkled with thousands of diamond-like crystals, and clung to the curves of her figure. It caressed her slender waist before flaring out into a full skirt sweeping around her feet. He had never seen anything so lovely.

Tamarith glanced across to where Jess and Dahll stood together. *Isn't it wonderful news about Jess?*

Vidarh smiled, remembering Jess's spate of sickness. She had been very apologetic when she'd told him, half-jokingly, that it hadn't been caused by his cooking after all.

He bent his head to kiss his new wife, holding her close.

They're both ecstatic, but just at this moment I don't think there is a happier person in the world than me.

Or me, Vidarh. She stood on tiptoe and gazed at him, her face aglow. *You know, in a strange way, we owe this day to Hedrohan. If she hadn't invaded Niflheim you wouldn't have come here, and we might never have met.*

Then I will never stop being grateful to her for that, even though she nearly killed me. Come. He took his bride by the hand, and led her to the cover of a small grove of trees. *I want to be alone with you again.*

She smiled and he kissed her again, tenderly and with great thoroughness. Afterward, he drew in a long, contented breath, as they stood in the moonlight, their arms entwined around each other.

"I love you, Vidarh," she said softly.

"And I you, Tamarith."

217

It came to him then, that he'd searched for this moment all of his life, without even knowing it. And it was here, in this moment and this place, that he belonged, in the beautiful settlement of Gladsheim, with the woman who had linked her mind and heart with his forever.

About the author...

I am intensely proud of being Welsh, although I currently reside in England with my husband Dave and three horses, Sally, Harry and T'pau. I have made up stories in my head for as long as I can remember, inspired by the beautiful Welsh scenery and its legends, and acting out my characters' roles in my mind.

I have always had three great loves—Horses, Reading and Writing, as well as being passionately fond of all animals and the outdoors. I enjoy writing Westerns, but my favourite genre is Science Fiction and Fantasy. I usually manage to have a horse somewhere in my stories, whatever the genre, and it did not take me long to realise that there was another essential element which would always occur in my stories—Romance with a capital 'R'.

I write the kind of stories I like to read: stories that take me, as a writer, into other worlds, where for a while I can forget the problems of the real world—and I hope they will do the same for my readers. Having given up my fulltime work as an administrator, I am now looking forward to being able to devote a lot more time to writing. My heroines are always strong but feminine, my heroes brave but caring...love will conquer all.

Contact Hywela at Lyn@Hywelalyn.co.uk

Visit Hywela at www.Hywelalyn.co.uk